Joe #
313 - 414 5185

True Confessions

True Confessions

Electa Rome Parks

Urban Books, LLC
78 East Industry Court
Deer Park, NY 11729

ISBN 13: 978-1-61129-201-5
Printed in the United States of America

Acknowledgments

Hey, family! What do you know good? We have been on this journey, together, for so many years now, I hold a special place in my heart for you. I have shared bits and pieces of my life with you and you guys have e-mailed me with bits and pieces of yours. Calling you "readers" is simply not enough. So, family it is. We have bonded over the years. LOL.

This is book #7. Wow! Can you believe it? I remember back to the days when all I had was an active imagination and a dream. And to this day, I still have an active imagination and a dream. LOL.

What's going on with me? Life is good. I made the decision to live my life like it's golden because it really is. We only come this way once and I intend to do all I can to make the most of it. I'm not where I want to be, but I'm having hella fun getting there. And, mainly, I'm claiming it across the universe. So, it's a done deal.

If you are reading these acknowledgments then you have a copy of *True Confessions* in your hand. Thank you, thank you, thank you for all your support! Your support and encouragement throughout the years have been priceless. I can't stress enough how important you, my readers, my family, are. Someone asked me in an interview what the best part of being an author was. I didn't hesitate or stutter. Hands down, besides

Acknowledgments

giving birth to my characters, meeting you guys is still awesome.

I obtain the same gratification I did the very first time I was in a bookstore and spotted a reader purchasing a copy of *The Lies That Bind*, my baby. My girlfriend and I literally started screaming, pointed at the book in her hand like two lunatics, and bum-rushed the reader. She didn't know what was going on until the store manager explained that I was the author, a highly enthusiastic new author. I still get a laugh out of that!

I know you guys are saying, "This isn't one of your blogs, so get to the point." Okay, okay, I will (smile). I cannot state enough how appreciative I am that you've brought my crazy, imperfect characters into your homes and embraced them as your own. Thank you! Thank you for giving my imagination, my characters, and my dream a place to thrive.

Special thanks to my family and friends: Thank you for putting up with my hermit-like state when I'm working on a manuscript and for simply allowing me to take time away from you to follow my passion. I love you guys much more than you will ever know and I wish the very best in life for each of you. Nelson, Brandon, Briana, Tresseler, Laymon, DaJuan, Jordan, Khai, my cousins and friends. You are my anchors. 'Cause you know Pisces always have our heads off in la-la land.

Many thanks to the many book clubs across the country who have welcomed me into your homes, phone lines, and conferences like welcoming a long-lost friend back into the fold. My characters become living and breathing creatures through your eyes. We talk about them as if they were. You guys are the best! Continue to be literary ambassadors and

Acknowledgments

continue to spread the word about my books. I appreciate it! Word of mouth is everything in this industry.

To my teams of literary greats, what would I do without you? Special thanks to: Ella Curry (you're the best), AALBC.com, MosaicBooks.com, APOOO, RAWSISTAZ, Disilgold.com, Black Expressions Book Club, Lip Service Ink, Cryus Webb, and the numerous blog radio stations that have hosted me. If I've missed anyone, you know what's in my heart, and know it wasn't intentional.

To my author friends, especially Cheryl Robinson and Cydney Rax, I am so honored to be your friend. We can literally talk for hours regarding this crazy world we've found ourselves caught up in. Isn't it fabulous? To all the authors who extended "acts of kindness" toward me this past year, I am so appreciative because you didn't have to (you know who you are). To all the authors I've met over the years, and there have been many, know that it is a privilege to possess the power of the pen. Words are powerful. You have the ability to create, destroy, and literally change lives. Don't underestimate your gift. I'm happy to be part of this elite membership.

Last, but definitely not least, to my publishing family: Portia (agent), Natalie, Brenda, and Diane, I haven't had the opportunity to meet you guys face-to-face yet but it has been a sincere pleasure working with you via our e-mail communications. I know . . . I ask a lot of questions and I'm impatient and I'm very detailed, oh, and picky, but we are all family and it's all good.

Family, please keep in touch. Drop me a line at

Acknowledgments

novelideal@aol.com. You know I love to hear from you. And yeah, I'm still sensitive about my stuff. Also, check me out at:

www.facebook.com/electaromeparks,
www.myspace.com/author_chick,
www.electaromeparkseblogspot.com,
and www.electaromeparks.com.

Until next time, I pray your life is filled with peace, joy, and hope. Remember there is only one thing greater than yourself . . .

Stay blessed,

Electa

SIGNING OFF, ATLANTA, APRIL 29, 2010:2:37 P.M.

Prologue

My reality is surreal and happens in super-slow motion. A nervous giggle escapes my chapped, dry, and parched lips. I lick them to restore moisture. Then, there is utter, deadly silence. If I listen closely, I can hear my heartbeat beating away at an accelerated pace. My senses are heightened and I marvel over the brilliant, bold colors of my bedroom as I inhale my favorite fragrances, from their spot on my antique dresser, colliding into one another with their potent allure. Even my sense of touch is different somehow. Everything is magnified to the nth degree. It's like I'm looking down at myself from a huge movie screen with surround sound as I ready myself for the big finale—the final shot and then fade to black.

I've never been good at saying good-bye, even on short weekend trips. I keep the handwritten note short and sweet and pray to God that Mother will understand, and, hopefully, one day forgive me.

I don't mean to hurt her or cause her any fresh pain. I sincerely don't. I hope she understands that this isn't her fault, that I love her with all my heart and being. No matter what, that fact will never change. I'm so thankful and forever grateful that she chose me to be her daughter out of all the orphaned babies in the world. She chose me. I told myself over and over again that that made me special. I needed to feel special instead of unwanted and discarded.

I'll miss Mother the most, but the hurt I feel inside is too unbearable and indescribable. It is too painful for me to continue, day in and day out, with just a hollow emptiness that erodes and corrupts any happiness that briefly surfaces. The dawn of each new day only brings me more heartache and renewed memories. Some memories are like leeches. They latch on for dear life and slowly, ever so slowly, suck and drain all the blood, all the living out of you. You are left with just a shell of the old you and that's no way to survive. Not for me, anyway.

When they find me, I want it to look like I'm sleeping, peacefully. Just like Sleeping Beauty who only needed a handsome prince to kiss her and awaken her from the darkness that engulfed her. However, for me, there won't be a handsome, charming prince to wake me, save me, and ride off into eternity. All my so-called princes were monsters in disguise with their hidden agendas that attempted to crush and stamp out my self-esteem. Yes, just blessed sleep awaits me.

I chose pills. I couldn't subject Mother to a messy, bloody scene that comes with slitting one's wrists or shooting one's self. I refuse to take my final breath with that heavy on my heart. I don't think my heart could handle anything else weighing against it. As it is, I feel like I have 300 pounds weighing me down, crushing the life out of me.

As I settle myself comfortably on my queen-sized bed, slowly pull the red satin comforter up to my chin, and stare at the full bottle of prescription pills carefully nestled in my right hand, I can't imagine not waking up in the morning.

What will it be like to not see the rising sun? To not hear my alarm clock going off announcing it's time to get ready for another day of work? Not hitting snooze to give myself another fifteen minutes? Not rushing to finish my morning rituals before I dash out the door and into rush-hour traffic? What will that feel like?

More important to me now, though, is will it hurt? I hope not. I have never been able to tolerate too much pain: physical, mental, or emotional. Yet, that's what Drake has caused me for the last year of my life. Pain. Intolerable suffering.

I only wanted to love him and for him to love me in return. Simple enough. Was that asking too much? My part of the equation was accomplished, effortless. Drake claimed he loved me, but he really didn't. Probably never could. Didn't know how to love or receive it. After what happened last week, I know he didn't. Yet, I gave him everything: my heart, my body, my soul. Now, I have nothing left to give myself. I'm empty inside.

As tears slowly flood my weary eyes and blur my vision, I look around my cozy bedroom for the last time. Ever. It used to be one of my favorite rooms in my small two-bedroom, one-bath apartment. There was nothing better than lighting several fragrant candles, drinking a little white wine, and cozying up with a good romance novel. Yes, that was heaven. Simple things excite me. Always have. Watching a sunrise or sunset, waking up to birds chirping in the treetops, walking hand in hand through the park with the one I love: all these things brought me great joy.

Mother will have to understand. I left her a note, propped up on the nightstand, in full view, that explains how much I love her and Daddy. What will she think when she can't reach me tonight? I would love to hear her soothing, loving voice one last time. Yet, I know I wouldn't be able to go through with my plan if I did. I'd give away my intentions over the phone or Mother would pick up on my foul mood and that would be that. I'd wake up another day with this aching, dull pain inside, tearing me apart, bit by bit. Pain that dulls and diminishes every ounce of my strength, all the way down to my pores.

Drake Collins. His name leaves a bitter taste on my tongue. Just the thought of him brings bile to the back of my throat. I will forever regret the day I met that man. If I could turn back the hands of time, do it all over again, I would have called in sick that day or run for the hills. I was just fine with my life the way it was. Sure, it wasn't exciting or glamorous, but it was enough for me. Drake came with the charm, movie-star looks, glitz, and high drama, and reeled me right in like a bass caught at sea. I gladly jumped into his net.

I say a silent prayer of forgiveness as I place one, then two colorful pills on my tongue and swallow dry. I didn't think of getting a glass of water. I can't think. The lump in my throat quickly diminishes. There's no turning back now. Just like there was no turning back when Drake turned me out. The countdown begins. *Ten, nine, eight* . . . I've lived a happy life. I have tons of good memories. I've treated others the way I wanted to be treated.

I hope this happens quickly. I steadfastly place three, four pills on my tongue and swallow again. Hot tears start to spill forth and stream down my cheeks as I realize the final result of my actions. *Seven, six, five* . . . It's for the best. I need to stop the pain. Will *he* even miss me? Or will he just move on to his next victim? Will all this be in vain?

I guess I'll never have that family now. The one I used to daydream and write about in my journal. The family with the almost perfect mommy and daddy and two kids: a boy and girl. The boy would be the oldest, and he'd look out for and protect his younger sister. They'd have cute, adorable names and they'd know they were wanted and loved and cherished by their parents. They'd never feel unwanted.

Four, three . . . I swallow a handful of pills this time. I've lost count of how many I've digested. As spittle escapes from my mouth, I gag. I wipe the overflow away with the back of my hand and keep right on shoving pills in my mouth until the orange-brown medicine bottle is empty. I look inside, in awe, shake the bottle, and can't believe the pills are gone so quickly. Just like the illusion of love. If you blink, you'll miss it.

I wonder if Drake even realizes how much I loved him. Now, I wait for blessed relief and peace to take away my hurt and pain. I'm so tired. I am tired of loving the wrong men. Tired of giving my all, coming up empty, and getting absolutely nothing back in return. Good sex isn't the end all to everything. Drake taught me that lesson.

Two, one . . . It won't be long now. I faintly smile and lie back against my down pillow. I welcome peace. In my mind, I start silently repeating Psalm 23. *I shall walk through the valley of death; I shall fear no evil, for thou art with me.* I'm so sleepy. I can barely keep my eyes open. I can feel myself giving in to the fog that slowly invades my mind. Maybe if I close my eyes for a few moments. Yeah, just rest them for a few minutes without seeing Drake's face behind my heavy eyelids.

Suddenly, I feel lightheaded, like I'm floating on a big, fluffy white cloud, bouncing up and down, giddy, with not a care in the world. This is a different sensation that I literally reach out my right hand to embrace and never let go of. Not a care in the world. Nothing matters but blessed, uneventful sleep. I close my tired, weary eyes as the countdown ends. Fade to black.

Chapter 1

"Kennedy, baby, you ate like a sick bird. Look at this. You left the majority of your food on your plate. This is not acceptable. Not acceptable at all. You need to eat more, dear, in order to get your strength back," Mother stated, lifting and retrieving the small bamboo food tray from my lap. She had even included a small vase of fresh, colorful flowers to brighten my day. Everyone who knew me knew I adored fresh-cut flowers of all shades and varieties. I would splurge on flowers the way some women treated themselves to a new outfit or shoes.

"I'm not really hungry, Mother," I declared, changing position and turning away with my back to her. I didn't want her to see the frustration that was clearly etched across my pinched, crunched-up face.

I understood she meant well, but I only ate as much as I did to please her. I didn't have an appetite, and I certainly didn't feel like talking. In fact, I didn't *feel* like doing anything but sleeping. I wanted to curl up in a tiny, tight ball, pull my covers over my head, and simply sleep my meaningless life away. Sleep was my comfort and salvation.

"Since when did you start leaving my famous scrambled eggs, grits, and country ham on your plate?"

I didn't bother to answer. I only pretended to be

sleepy as I faked a wide-mouthed yawn. I didn't even bother to cover my mouth with my hand.

"Usually, by now, you are on your second helping," Mother volunteered, picking up a few discarded clothes from the floor and placing them in the hamper.

"I don't know what's going on. I'm kinda tired. I think I'm going to nap for a while."

Even though I didn't see her face, I knew Mother was staring at me with that worried expression on her butter-pecan face. It was the expression she tried so hard to disguise when I was looking directly at her.

"Baby, that is not acceptable. You just woke up. You've only been awake a little over an hour. We have a beautiful day ahead of us and you can't spend it sleeping all day." To prove her point, Mother strolled over to my bedroom window and boldly opened my mini blinds so that the early morning sunlight greeted me with a blinding, direct glare.

I groaned and shielded my eyes with the back of my hand.

"Here, sit up," she commanded, attempting to fluff up my down pillows, and gently propping them behind my back. She reached for the journal that sat on my nightstand.

"Why don't you write in your journal for a while?" she asked, holding it out to me like she was offering a piece of candy to a small child.

"Mother, I really don't—"

"That nice doctor said that writing down your thoughts would help you, be therapeutic. Help you come to grips with this, uh, this situation. Here. Take this and let me go and find you a pen. Or do you prefer a pencil?"

"A pen is fine, Mother."

Reluctantly, I sat up completely and resigned myself to writing in my new journal. Actually, I had kept journals in the past, especially during my college days when life was so new and exciting. I wrote everything down. Up until that point, I had led a somewhat sheltered life.

Reading and writing were major parts of my life; at least, they were before Drake. Reading took me to places I had never been and enabled me to meet bold and exciting new friends. In my books, female heroines did and said things I could only imagine and read about. They were powerful. Something that I wasn't.

Maybe if I pleased Mother, cooperated, and pretended to feel better, she would go home, back across town to her townhome, sooner rather than later.

Today was my first full day back home from the hospital and Mother decided on her own that she'd move in with me and nurse me back to my old self. The problem was that I didn't know if I wanted to go back to my previous existence. I didn't like the old me.

"There you go, baby," she said, walking back into the room and handing me the Uni-ball purple pens I adore.

"Thank you."

"You entertain yourself and I'm going to clean up around here until lunchtime. What do you feel like eating today? I know you are glad to be away from that nasty hospital food."

I shrugged my shoulders because I really didn't care. Food was the furthest thing from my mind at the moment.

That didn't derail Mother; she continued to chitchat. "What about a nice salad and a baked chicken breast?"

"That's fine." I attempted to offer a smile.

Mother seemed pleased as she ran her hand across

my dresser top. "You really should dust around here. Got dust bunnies everywhere. I found one behind your sofa that was big as a small cat. You know I didn't raise you like that."

"Okay, could you shut my bedroom door behind you? Please?"

There it was again. That look. I saw that look flash across her pretty face again. Just for a quick moment, a second. If you weren't careful, you'd miss it. That look that said she was afraid to close the door. Afraid of what I might do to myself behind closed doors. Frightened I might try to hurt myself again.

"Mother, I'll be fine. I promise. I'll call you if I need anything." I even managed a faint, small smile again.

Hesitantly, Mother left my bedroom and closed my door, with an inch left ajar. That inch spoke silent volumes. I heard her moving around in my living room and tiny kitchen. Drawers were opened and closed. Water was run in the kitchen sink. I lay back and closed my eyes as I felt that familiar blackness attempt to engulf me; completely overtake me. I pulled my comforter around me like a cocoon of protection and security. My temples were throbbing.

Meanwhile, in the living room, the vacuum cleaner started up, with Mother humming loudly in the background. Crooning one of her favorite tunes, "Amazing Grace". Then, I heard the familiar sounds of a morning talk show coming on. There was definitely no sleeping now. I looked down and once again examined my brand-new leather journal and thought *why not*. It had tons of blank, lined pages to write on. Maybe if I wrote some of my thoughts down, I could make some sense of the turn my life had taken. But where to begin? I remembered a college professor telling us that every story has a beginning, middle, and ending. Simple enough. I'd start at the beginning.

Chapter 2

My name is Kennedy and I'm a coward. Coward. Such a small, simple six-letter word. A word that has applied to me for most of my life. I know I'm a coward. Always have known. I accept that fact just like I accept air to breathe for my very existence. I've been afraid of so many things during my twenty-eight years of life. Ask Mother and she'll tell you how, as a child, I was afraid of spiders, snakes, rats, hairy monsters, and, the biggest one of all, the dark. Like most children, I was a big scaredy cat when it came to dealing with those imagined or unimagined fears and things that go bump in the night.

For most people, when we become adults, our fears subside. Not me. I'm still afraid. I'm terrified of not being loved. I'm afraid of not being wanted. Of saying the wrong things. I'm afraid of showing my true nature. I'm afraid of saying no and standing up for myself. Bottom line, I'm petrified of living life to the fullest for fear of someone disapproving. And that's how all my problems begin and end. Plain and simple, I'm a coward because I realize these things and won't do anything about them. It's easier to turn a deaf ear and hope they'll magically go away. Not.

Don't let anyone tell you any different. It's easier to take your life than to deal with your reality. Taking

your life, committing suicide, doesn't take an ounce
of courage. The courage is in living and tackling your
issues head on.

I guess you've figured it out by now. I survived my
suicide attempt—thanks to Mother. You see, she calls
me every Sunday night at exactly seven o'clock P.M. on
the dot. Rain or shine. She never fails. You can set your
watch by her, almost to the second. We use this time
to catch up on our individual weeks, even though we
don't live that far from one another. The majority of the
time, it is Mother who goes on and on about something
or another. I usually listen and make a comment here
and there to let her know she still has my captive,
undivided attention.

I consumed the bottle of pills at approximately
6:45 P.M. Talk about a pathetic case of crying out for
help. Could I have been any more obvious? When the
cordless phone sitting on my nightstand started to
ring at exactly seven o'clock P.M., I couldn't ignore it.
With each ring, the noise became louder and louder as
it wracked my nerves to no end. I just had to pick up
the receiver and hear her voice one last time. By seven
o'clock, I was slipping fast into an unconscious state,
but I had enough strength to murmur a faint greeting.

You can figure out most of the rest. As I had predicted,
even through my haze, when I heard Mother's voice, I
told her everything the best I could in my foggy state of
mind. I stumbled on about Drake and how unworthy,
undesirable, and unhappy he made me feel.

Mother kept me talking, awake, sent help, and saved
my life. She was able to dial 911 on her cell as she talked
and listened to me on her home phone. The doctor
on call in the emergency room pumped my stomach,

and then I rested as comfortably as I could for the remainder of the night.

I vaguely recall Mother faithfully by my side, holding my hand and uttering soothing words in between her muffled, hidden sobs. I turned my head away because I couldn't bear to see the sadness in her brown eyes, unhappiness that I had placed there. The nurse asked who Drake was because she said I called out for him a few times in my fretful sleep. I dreamt of darkness, pain, suffering, and the devil coming to take me away. I awoke in a cold sweat, shaking, and a scream on the tip of my tongue.

Through it all, or at least the parts I can partially recall, I wondered what he, Drake, would think of my failed attempt at taking my own life. He was constantly reminding me how I never completed anything, outside of work. I'd start a project and never see it through to completion, or I'd have so many different things going on at one time that I could never give 100 percent to any one task. Oh well, I guess this is the perfect example of not completing a project. I am alive and breathing, even if I am not well.

Chapter 3

Day two after my suicide attempt was spent in the hospital. I was a bit more coherent, even though I didn't want to speak with or see anyone. If I had had the power to disappear, I would have. All I desired was to burrow under my drab hospital sheets and sob. However, I couldn't cry because that would upset Mother too much and she'd start crying. It pained me to see her upset. Over the last few years, Mother has shed enough tears for the both of us. She took her divorce pretty hard, but that's another story for a different time.

The hospital sent their in-house psychiatrist to visit me. He was an older white man with the bluest eyes I'd ever seen. His eyes reminded me of the tropical waters of Jamaica; you could get lost in them. He was rather animated and talked with his hands. He dropped by and asked a ton of questions about what I was feeling, took a lot of notes on a yellow legal pad, and eventually gave me a business card with the name of a psychiatrist for me to see after I was released. Dr. Mitchell, (I think that was his name) suggested I start keeping a journal to help sort out my thoughts and deepest feelings. Before exiting my room, he gently squeezed my shoulder, gave me a sympathetic smile, and that was that.

Mother was acting so strange, like this never happened. Like it was all an unintentional act. Like I accidentally swallowed a bottle full of prescription pills. I may be a coward, but Mother is afraid of handling things. If it is something she doesn't want to address, she will act like it doesn't exist. Case in point, my attempted suicide. If ignoring that brought her peace, so be it.

No one knew what happened to me at my job as a senior relations service representative for a telecommunications company. You know what? Even if they had known, they probably wouldn't have cared. I pretty much went to work, performed my job responsibilities, and went home. I had not accumulated many friends in the three years I'd been there. As far as they knew or were told, and this included my manager, I had been out sick for a few days. That was believable, because lately the flu had been going around and everybody was catching the bug.

Drake.

Drake. I never wanted to set my eyes on him for the rest of my life. If I never, ever saw him, that would be too soon. I don't know what led me to believe that I'd make a difference in his life and he'd fall hopelessly and helplessly in love with me. What made me think that I'd possess him someday? Drake could never be possessed by a mere woman. I think he secretly hates the female population and only tolerates and uses us for his enjoyment and pleasure.

Chapter 4

Day three after my suicide attempt had me being released from the hospital, and going home to an empty apartment with an even emptier life. Still pretending everything was peachy keen, Mother had cleaned up my apartment, stocked my refrigerator with nutritious, healthy organic foods, thrown out every bottle of pills I had in my medicine cabinet, and even had a homecoming gift waiting for me: a leather-bound, tan, lined journal with hundreds of pages to fill with my confessions.

Dr. Mitchell may be right. If I write my feelings down, maybe I can make sense of my life as it's laid out in front of me in black and white. The only way to do that was to start from the beginning. What was that quote? The past holds the clues to your present.

Like Mother, I could pretend too. I could pretend to feel better because there was no way that I was going to visit that shrink and get a crazy label attached to me. I'm not wacky; I simply had a momentary lack of judgment due to depression. However, I was determined to make a fresh start without Drake in my life and in my dreams.

Chapter 5

Dear Journal,

I should start by telling you something about myself. Let's see. There's really not much to tell, not that's interesting anyway. I'm pretty average in most ways and live a relatively tame lifestyle. I'm twenty-eight years old. Work as a senior relations service representative for a telecommunications company in Midtown. By the way, it's a job I despise with a major passion, but I do my best nevertheless. It could be a cool job, but there is always so much drama going on with the women there. Trivial stuff at that. Why can't women just get along?

Oh, I'm adopted. Mother and Daddy adopted me when I was two months old. I was born to a crack-addicted biological mother who simply gave me up at birth. Signed over her maternal rights. Just like that. With the snap of two fingers. In the blink of an eye. She signed over her maternal rights, and I became a ward of the state of Georgia. She wasn't even sure who my biological father was. That line on my birth certificate was left blank. Recently, more and more, I have thought about hiring a detective agency to locate my birth mother because I have many questions. I even researched a few agencies online in the metro Atlanta area but I haven't made a decision, mainly because I don't want to hurt Mother.

I don't get it. And believe me, I've tried. How can a mother, any mother, give birth to a child she has carried for nine months, felt her moving around inside her, bonded with, and then, then . . . just give her up like she's dumping the trash? Me, I could never do that in a million years. It's actually ironic, my life didn't mean anything to my biological mother and I guess it didn't mean anything to me either since I tried to take it.

Luckily for me, Mother and Daddy came into my life when I was two months old. Mother said she took one look at me lying all alone in the hospital crib, underweight because I was born premature, and knew she had to have me to love, shield, and nurture. Mother said she'd never forget how small, fragile, and vulnerable I appeared. Like I was calling out for her to love and protect me. And she did and hasn't stopped loving me in all my twenty-eight years.

What else? I guess you could say I'm a loner. As I stated before, I don't have many friends, male or female. That's fine with me. I've halfway attempted to be friends with women at work, but in the end, there are too many jealousies, insecurities, and backstabbings going on. Mother said I shouldn't stress or worry about it. She claims these women are jealous of my good looks. I don't know, I think I have average looks. I'm about five feet seven, *very fair skinned, long, naturally wavy brownish-red hair, hazel eyes, and a slim frame. Mother is always saying I could be a model with my long legs, slim waist, and exotic looks.*

Anyhow, whatever the reason, I choose to go to work, do my job, and leave. My coworkers wrongly assume I'm a snob since I won't get involved in their gossip, after-work activities, and petty ways. Until a year ago, most weekends found me at home curled up with a good book.

Occasionally, Taylor, a college friend, would convince me to hit a local nightspot with her. I'd tag along to please her, even though the club scene wasn't really me. Clubbing wasn't my thing. Typically, I'd sit in the corner for most of the night, nurse one drink, and turn down dances left and right. Taylor, on the other hand, lived on the dance floor and loved the attention men showered on her.

I've never been good with men, either. I've never had problems attracting men, only with attracting the right ones. I honestly think I have an invisible sign posted on my forehead that says: **USE AND ABUSE ME. PLEASE.** *The wrong ones flock to me like bees to honey.*

After I met Drake, I thought all that had changed, that it was all in my past. I felt like I had won the lottery and I had the chance for love, marriage, and a family. How wrong I was. Love is so blind. It feels right, even when it's wrong.

Looking back, Drake knew exactly how to make me feel good; sexually, that is.

***

"Ohhh yeah, baby. That's right. Don't stop doing what you're doing." Drake was in heaven.

"Okay, babe. Anything you say. You sure you can handle this?" I teased in between licks.

Starting in small circles, I twirled my tongue up and down his shaft and with each flick reached farther and farther out. When I placed all of him inside my warm mouth, I thought Drake was going to collapse in a heap in the middle of the floor.

"Damn, Kennedy. You do that shit too good," he exclaimed as his eyes rolled back in his head like he was going into convulsions.

"Who do you love?" I asked, momentarily pausing to look up at him. I needed to hear him say it, again.

"Don't stop now. Put it back in. I was almost there. Put it in," Drake moaned, trying to place his stiff, massive organ back in the comfort and warmth of my eager, accommodating mouth.

"No, not until you answer my question," I stated, shyly looking up at him from beside the sofa in my living room.

"Damn, Kennedy, you can't tease a man like this," he exclaimed, pushing my long hair back out of my flushed face. Unsuccessfully, he tried to force my head back down with his other hand.

"Who do you love?" I asked determinedly.

I took the opportunity to suck down on his tip, just like he had taught me. Not too hard, but with enough pressure to cause him to involuntarily shudder and close his eyes. Drake had patiently and expertly instructed me on everything he liked *me to do to him in bed. The things I didn't care for, I did them anyway. Just to please him. Cosmopolitan magazine articles revealed that what you wouldn't do for your man, another woman would. Women should learn to be accommodating in the bedroom. I went above and beyond for Drake.*

Tonight was costume night. Sometimes Drake and I played these games where I'd dress up in costumes and live out his fantasies. It kept the sex exciting and interesting, is what Drake said. I had no complaints. Tonight, I had on this red and blue cheerleading outfit minus the panties and bra. I even sported long socks and tennis shoes to complete the look.

As I squatted on the floor with my open, bent legs, Drake manually stimulated me and squeezed my breasts through the fabric while I pleased him. My wetness was all over his fingers. I think I was addicted to his dick; it was beautiful just like him, and I could suck him for hours.

"Kennedy, baby. You know I love you. From the first day I saw you, I've loved you," he exclaimed, rubbing some more on my spot. I felt my knees getting weak.

I let out a slow, sensual moan, closed my eyes and bit down on my bottom lip. "Yeah, right there." I opened my legs even wider, granting Drake full access.

He reached to push my head back down, and I searched his face for the truth. I knew Drake sometimes told me what he thought I wanted to hear. His confessions, sometimes, didn't hold an ounce of truth.

"Come on, baby. Work my dick. Do it like I taught you. Suck that lollipop."

"Hmmm, you taste sweet," I cooed, licking my lips.

"It was love at first sight when you walked through my door. I knew you were the one."

Drake had told me all I needed to hear. His words were music to my soul. I went to work, harder and faster than before. How many licks does it take to get to the center of the Tootsie Roll Pop? Slurping, wet sounds echoed throughout the stillness of the moment. We never made love with any background music or noise. Drake was turned on by the sensual, raw sounds and smells of our lovemaking.

"Oh, yeah. That's it. That's my girl. Damn," he screa-med out in ecstasy as I moved just in time before he spewed all over me. With his eyes still closed and a big smile on his gorgeous face, Drake collapsed against my sofa, pulled me to him, and caressed my hair and face over and over. He loved to run his hands through my wavy locks. Drake despised when I wore my hair pulled up in a ponytail, and he expected me to take it down when I was with him. I obliged. I was always accommodating.

"You're getting better. Go get a warm washcloth for your man," he said, pulling up my skirt and smacking me on the ass two times, leaving a light red mark.

I stared at him from my spot on the floor. Getting better? I thought he'd enjoyed that. I knew he did. I was on point with all he had taught me. I made a mental note to do better the next time. I had finally gotten my gag reflex under control. Maybe next time I'd surprise him by swallowing.

"Go on, baby. Hurry up," he demanded, bending down from the sofa and taking one of my throbbing nipples in his mouth like he possessed it, and absently playing between my quivering legs. "I'm ready to eat some honey because your pussy always tastes like some."

I quickly jumped up to retrieve a towel because I knew what was in store for me. My kitty twitched. Twitched again. Drake was off the chain when it came to sexing me. He had turned me out; inside and out.

In my daze, I glanced around and surveyed my surroundings. In my bed, safe and sound in my tiny apartment. The ringing telephone woke me from my flashback of events that had transpired several months earlier, during happier times. The tingling between my legs was present day and very real. My coochie was having some serious dick withdrawals and feeling like an addict, craving a piece of Drake. However, that would happen only over my dead body.

Chapter 6

"Hello . . . Kennedy is not available to come to the phone right now. She's sleeping . . . No, I will not wake her up. I don't care who this is . . . What? Drake, why don't you leave my daughter alone? It's obvious you aren't good for her. You don't care about my daughter and you never have . . . Well, Kennedy will always be my little girl . . . I've already told you. Good-bye, Drake. Don't call here again."

I didn't even realize another day had shown its face until I awoke to Mother screaming. Well, not exactly screaming, but speaking in an extremely high, agitated voice to someone on the phone. When I realized it was Drake, I became fully alert and awake as my heart did a tap dance and pitter-patter before flip-flopping a couple of times.

I wanted to speak with him, but then on the other hand, I feared what he'd say to me and how I'd react. Being with Drake had always been a contradiction to my emotions. He took me, like no other, to extreme highs or devastating lows.

"Mother. Please come here," I screamed loud enough for her to hear me in the living room.

"Yes, baby?" she asked, slowly walking back into my room with a puzzled, worried expression on her face.

"Who was that on the phone? I heard you talking to someone."

"Oh, no one baby. It was a wrong number."

We stared at each other, eyeball to eyeball, for a few seconds. Both of us recognized the lie in her words and gestures. The untruth clung to the air like stale cigar smoke.

"Oh, I see. Why don't you put the phone back in my room today? I'm feeling much stronger."

"No, you don't need that annoyance. I can answer your calls for a few more days. You need to rest."

"Mother, it's not like my friends are blowing up my phone line."

"Well, for now, let me answer it. Let your mother do for you. Honestly, I don't mind," she stated, smoothing the comforter on my bed with her hand.

"Okay, if it'll make you feel better," I stated reluctantly.

"It will. Oh, before I forget, Taylor called you last night."

"Did she? Where was I?"

"Knocked out. I didn't have the heart to wake you. You were sleeping so peacefully after dinner."

"I guess I was more tired than I realized."

"Your doctor said it would be a few days until your strength returned."

"Was there a message?"

"No, she said she'd try back later."

"Okay."

"Anyway, I was just going to wake you, so I'm glad you're up. Perfect timing. I've run you a nice, hot bath with your favorite bubble bath. After your bath, I'll have your breakfast ready and I thought maybe we could eat in the dining room."

"I'd rather eat in here."

"No. You need to get up and about. It'll do your soul good, Kennedy."

"Mother, I don't feel—"

She held up her hand. "Kennedy, I don't want to discuss it any further. Now, let me go and prepare our breakfast. I'd like for you to get up. Now."

"Sure. All right," I stated in resignation. "Mother, thanks for running my bath water."

"You're welcome, baby," she said, turning to leave.

"Mother?"

"Yes, honey?"

"If Drake calls, I would like to speak with him."

Mother started to protest, but I stopped her this time before she could continue.

"Mother, I want to speak with him." I didn't dare mention how I *needed* to speak with him. "Okay?"

She didn't answer, just continued to walk out with a stiff back.

"Mother?" I called out again.

She paused in mid-stride, but didn't turn around. I barely heard her next words.

"Kennedy, I heard you the first time."

Chapter 7

Dear Journal,

It's already day three of my discharge from the hospital and today has been very productive for me. I feel somewhat stronger, physically anyway. I got out of bed and dressed, plus I plan to call my best friend Taylor back. She always places a genuine smile on my face and sometimes I wish I could be more like her. I envy the carefree way she breezes through life. Her motto is: "Life is too short not to live it to its fullest."

Right now, I am really pissed at Mother. In fact, internally, I am simmering. Mother thinks I'm a little girl with no mind of my own. I am not a child. I'm a twenty-eight-year-old grown woman and I wish she would wake up and realize that. Mother can't continue to go through life trying to protect me from everybody or everything that she deems evil or unsuitable. She has a good heart and means well, but she has to realize I have to learn to fight my own battles. Mother can't conquer them for me.

I can't believe she refused to let Drake talk to me earlier this morning. From what I heard, she even raised her voice to him, and Mother rarely raises her voice to anyone. She just nags, nags,

nags. She is the queen of nagging. Even when she and Daddy were going through their divorce, I never heard her screaming or shouting at him. Now, crying was another story. I heard plenty of sobbing and witnessed many tears shed. However, that was water under the bridge because they have both gone on with their separate lives.

Mother is fully in charge of her life now and has been since she and Daddy divorced over five years ago. During their long marriage, she doted on Daddy so much that she almost smothered him to death. She had good intentions, but it was suffocating to him. He said Mother choked the life out of him slowly but surely. One day, out of the blue, he simply left. According to Daddy, he couldn't take any more. Now, I receive that unorthodox love from her. Up until now, living in separate households made it bearable.

I knew it was a mistake telling Mother some of the cruel comments Drake had said to me. Sometimes I would start talking, without thinking, and all the negative emotions and feelings would flow freely from my loose tongue. Two Sundays ago, Mother caught me during one of those rare moments on the phone. I didn't tell her everything, but I told her enough, too much in fact. Now, she can't stand Drake's ass. If she knew the entire story, she'd want to kill him with her bare hands.

Let me tell you about the man I loved. Notice "love" is past tense. Drake is such a handsome man. He has movie-star good looks and can have any woman he desires. Yet, he chose me. In the beginning I was flattered, then I realized he sensed

*something vulnerable in me that he could control.
Drake thrives on control and he's an expert at iden-
tifying a person's weaknesses. That is something I
would learn further down the line.*

*The first time I set eyes on Drake was a year,
two months, and a day ago. I can break it down to
the hours, minutes, even seconds if you asked me
to because I recall it just like it was yesterday. If
only I had known or sensed in some way that he'd
be trouble. Trouble with a capital T. If it's too good
to be true, then it probably is, and all that glitters
isn't gold. Drake was more like fool's gold.*

*I was delivering business reports and corre-
spondence up to the sixth floor to one of the managers, Bill Walker. Mr. Walker managed some
of the top-tier clients that I serviced. We were
engaged in the usual cordial how's-the-weather
chitchat in his spacious office. Not much of anything was really being said. Then Mr. Walker
asked me the question that changed my entire
life—for the worse.*

*"Kennedy, have you met our new manager,
Drake Collins? He came to us by way of California
roughly two weeks ago."*

"No, I haven't."

*"Well, come and let me introduce the two of
you. You'll probably work with him periodically
on accounts and assist in getting him up to speed."*

*We walked out of Mr. Walker's corner office
and strolled four doors over. I envied management. They all had large, stately offices that had
floor-to-ceiling windows and were privileged to a
spectacular view of Atlanta and could see as far*

away as Stone Mountain. Me, I had a tiny cubicle that didn't have a door I could conveniently close for privacy, and I definitely didn't have a view of the city. My view was the grayish wall of my cubbyhole.

With my degree in business administration I could be in management, but I didn't have the desire to play the political games that were necessary to be successful in corporate America. Honestly, I didn't know what I wanted to do.

Whenever I complained to Mother, she encouraged me to go back to school for my MBA. Sometimes I thought it was a good idea, but other times I wasn't feeling another two or more years of professors, studying, and exams. With a full-time job, when would I have the time or energy?

As we walked into Mr. Collins's office, sitting with his back to us and talking on the phone was an African American male who spoke with authority and power. He signaled with his finger that he would be just a moment. We patiently waited for him to end his phone call, and I quickly checked out his office space with curiosity.

Everything was neat, in place, and very efficient looking. There were not a lot of personal items such as photos or anything of that nature. So, I wasn't sure if he was married or had any children. This new manager had a few colorful framed prints and affirmations on his wall and credenza. I still hadn't gotten a good look at Mr. Collins, but I was secretly thinking about all the work waiting for me.

Finally, he turned around and stood up to

address us, and I stumbled head first into his soulful eyes. Standing before me was the absolute most gorgeous man I had ever seen in my entire life. My breath caught in my throat. He was almost flawless; almost too perfect. Drake was the perfect specimen of a strong black man, on the outside anyway. The only imperfection I saw was a small scar, barely noticeable, right below his perfect bottom lip. I wanted to reach out, touch his cheek, and see if he was real, because the man standing before me had to be an illusion.

He was a six-foot-two god with slightly wavy close-cropped hair, light brown eyes, smooth dark brown skin, and a thin mustache that framed his beautiful smile. Even through his business jacket, I could make out the six-pack that was beneath his dress shirt. It was obvious he worked out at a gym because he was tight. I figured he was around thirty, no older than thirty-three. Yes, he was all man because just his presence was affecting me.

I was truly shocked that I hadn't heard the women on my floor talking, gossiping, and placing claims on this manly specimen. You couldn't miss Drake. When he walked in a room, he was the kind of man who made you pause in whatever you were doing and just drool. He commanded attention. I had merely blocked out my coworkers' comments regarding him, or maybe they hadn't bothered to inform me about him. I know they didn't consider me competition, not because of my looks, but because they knew I didn't date on the job.

*I didn't believe in office romances. I had wit-
nessed what messing with the boss could do for
you—give you your walking papers when the
relationship went south, or maybe an internal
black ball followed you out the door. Yes, the ter-
mination of office affairs had ended some promising careers at my company.*

*"Kennedy, Kennedy?" Mr. Walker repeated,
giving me an odd look with a slight smile on his
pale face.*

*Mr. Walker was forever in need of a few hours
of sun, but he was pretty decent. He always treated
me with respect and valued my opinion regarding clients. Recently, he personally called and
asked me why I hadn't interviewed for one of the
management positions that were open. Internal
associates always received first priority over
external candidates. Mr. Walker thought I was
a perfect candidate to interview for the position.*

*"Oh, I'm sorry," I said, swallowing the lump
that had suddenly formed in my throat. "I spaced
out for a moment. I guess I was thinking about
the workload waiting on my desk."*

*"Well, yes. You guys have been swamped with a
high volume of calls lately, since we installed the
new software. Don't worry, Drake and I won't
keep you long."*

*Drake and I awkwardly stared at each other. I
longed to hear what his voice would sound like directed toward me. I thought it would be rich, deep,
and sexy. Suddenly, images of him whispering sweet
nothings in my ear clouded my brain. What was
going on?*

"As I was saying, Kennedy, I'd like for you to meet Drake Collins. Drake, this is Kennedy Logan. She's one of our best senior relations service representatives. Kennedy has helped me out on numerous occasions and has an excellent rapport with many of our top-tier clients. She's a great asset to the company."

I held out my slightly shaky hand and tried, un-successfully, to stop the huge blush that had assaulted my face. I was pretty light skinned, so I knew that Drake and Mr. Walker noticed the redness that flushed my cheeks, neck, and face.

"Nice to meet you, Mr. Collins. Welcome aboard."

"Same here, nice to meet you too," he stated as his huge hand swallowed mine. I couldn't help but notice the contrast of our skin tones as they meshed in a handshake. I observed that Drake had perfectly manicured nails. And his hands, they were smooth and soft to the touch. I knew then that this man took care of himself and hadn't done any hard labor a day in his life. He had been pampered and catered to.

Even though we were in a professional setting, I saw Drake quickly and discreetly take me in from head to toe. Starting at my feet, Drake swiftly admired my long legs, paused at my hips, made his way up to my chest, and finally took in my glowing face. All in a matter of seconds. When I went out with Taylor, this was the same look that I typically received from the men in the clubs. In the clubs, it turned me off because I always felt I was being sized up like a piece of raw meat by the hungry lions. For some reason, with Drake, my

*heart gave a quick flutter. This completely caught
me off guard.*

*"Kennedy. What a lovely name." My name just
flowed off his tongue like a fine wine poured into
expensive crystal glassware.*

"Thank you."

"Are you originally from Atlanta, Kennedy?"

*"Yes, born and raised here. I am a true Georgia
peach."*

*"I can't believe it. I'm finding it's rare to find a
true Atlanta native. Everyone here seems to be a
transplant from New York, Florida, or someplace
up North."*

"Well, you've found me."

"Indeed I did."

He smiled.

I smiled.

*"Maybe you can suggest some good restaurants
for lunch and dinner, for that matter. I just relo-
cated from Los Angeles, and I'm still learning my
way around and finding the hot spots in the city."*

*"I'm afraid I'm the wrong one to ask. I usually
eat lunch at my desk. I'm a diehard brown bagger,"
I explained. Drake's eyes never left mine. I could
get lost in them. Drown. When the sunlight from
his open window blinds hit them just right, the
specks of green in his eyes danced around in merry
circles.*

*When we heard Mr. Walker politely clear his
throat, we came back to reality. As I brushed my
wild hair out of my face, I quickly blushed again
and looked down at the floor. Suddenly, I wished
I had worn my nice black Donna Karan suit and*

put on some makeup. Plus, I was in dire need of a manicure. I quickly balled my fingers into tight fists at my sides and hoped he hadn't noticed.

"Well, Miss Kennedy. It is Miss, isn't it?"

"Yes." I wanted to scream out, Yes, I'm single. Single and available. It had been awhile since I'd been in a long-term relationship. Any relationship.

"It's a pleasure to meet you, and I may have to call you so you can explain to me some of these reports you guys generate in your department. And if Bill recommended you, then you must be great," he said, holding my hand again, a bit too long. I shuddered and felt a moisture that surprised me.

"Nice meeting you too, and I'll be glad to explain the client reports. They can be a bit confusing to someone not used to reviewing them. Just give me a call. I'm in the directory, extension 3-5123."

"I may certainly do that," he said, releasing his hand and eyes from mine. My heart finally stopped fluttering, slowly returning to near normal.

As Mr. Walker and I walked out, I felt Drake's eyes as they seductively caressed my butt. When I discretely glanced back, our eyes meshed, I was lost, and he smiled. I offered a weak one in return and kept walking, faster. Somebody was a lucky woman because I knew that man had a woman. And if she was smart, she was a woman who kept a close eye on him. As Taylor would say, "Don't shit where you eat."

Drake could almost make a woman go back on her promise to never date someone she worked with.

***

Later that evening, after a somewhat tense day with Mother, I decided to give Taylor a quick call. I didn't feel like talking, but I knew if I didn't call her back, I'd get sixty questions later on. And I had no intention of telling her of my attempt to take my life. Sure, she was my best friend, but I was a private person to a fault. There were some things even Taylor didn't know about me. Many things she probably never will.

She was always complaining that she told me all her business and I consistently held out on her. Not that there was much to tell on my end. Taylor, on the other hand, always had an exciting story to share. I told her that she needed to write a book or two. Relationship stories with lots of drama were bestsellers.

I dialed Taylor's phone number from memory, and lay back against my bed pillow. It was raining lightly outside and I could feel the gloom trying to pull me back in and consume me. I had lit a couple of my favorite candles to give my room a nice, fragrant smell. Lately, it smelled stuffy and confining. I realized I was going stir crazy; the walls were closing in on me and my random thoughts.

Mother and I had shared an uncommonly quiet dinner. I knew what was bothering her even if she wouldn't admit it. She didn't want me to talk with Drake or have anything else to do with him. And I could understand her feelings, but I couldn't make that promise to her, not just yet. I couldn't make the promise to myself. So, Mother tried not to confront me, and I tried not to upset her anymore than I already had. Therefore, dinner was quiet and subdued and strained. Each of us was lost in our own personal thoughts as we ate shrimp linguini, a garden salad, and rolls, and drank iced tea.

***

"Hello?"

"Hey, girl," I said, trying to sound as cheerful as possible.

"Oh, so you finally call back your best friend? Where have you been? I've been calling and calling for two days now. Images of your dead and rotting body were running through my mind," she said, releasing that high-pitched, cheery laughter of hers. Taylor was always in a good mood. I could probably count on one hand the number of times I'd seen her in a foul mood. Me, I was another story. I thought that Taylor didn't know how close she was to the truth about me being dead.

"I haven't been feeling well. I had to go to the emergency room the other night."

"What? What happened? Why didn't you call me?" she asked with concern etched in her voice.

"No, Mother came by, took control as usual, and drove me to the hospital."

"You still could have called; I am your best friend," she pouted. "What's the verdict?"

"Nothing much. I caught the flu and had gotten severely dehydrated." I surprised myself at how convincely the lies rolled off my tongue.

"Better you than me. You should have gotten a flu shot."

"Thanks a lot."

"Girl, you know I'm kidding." She chuckled.

"I'm not so sure."

"Can I bring you anything? Soup? Orange juice?"

"No, I'm cool."

"Well, how are you feeling now?"

"Better."

"Is that why Mrs. Logan is over there? She answered my call last night."

"Yeah, Mother is nursing me back to health. You know how she is; this is right up her alley."

"Well then, I know you are in good hands. It's sickening the way that woman dotes on you. Gives you anything you want and then some."

"Whatever."

"I'm not hatin'. Girl, you got it made."

"I guess."

"You guess? You know how my mom and I just co-exist. Consider yourself lucky to have a mother who puts your needs before her own."

"You're right and I do count my blessings."

"But you are feeling better?"

"Yes, a little."

"Good, because you have to go with me to the club this weekend. I've already bought this tight, sexy black dress and shoes. Cost me a small fortune."

"I don't know, Taylor. You know how I hate that entire club scene."

"I know, but you need to get out now that you and Drake have broken up. He can't stop you from going out with me anymore."

Just the mention of Drake's name momentarily sped up my heart. I burrowed deeper into my pillow, exhausted.

"Are you there? Can you hear me?"

"Yeah, I'm here."

"Well? You still are broken up, aren't you? Don't tell me you've gotten back together," she questioned cautiously.

"Yes," I answered, cutting her off. "We are still broken up."

"Well, is it a go for this weekend?" Taylor asked.

"First of all, Drake didn't stop me from going to the club with you when we were dating. I wanted to spend time with him because he was always out of town on business."

"Yeah, right. Tell me anything, K. Quit making excuses for that man. You know Drake was always trying to tell you what to do and you usually listened. You did what he said, period. I've witnessed it with my own eyes and it made me sick to my stomach."

"Whatever, Taylor. Just drop it."

"I am going to drop it because I don't want to upset you. So, are we hanging out?"

"I don't like feeling like I'm on display. I only go to hang out with you; do you a favor and spend time with my best friend."

"Maybe you'll meet a nice man."

"I'm not looking for one."

"I know, because you definitely didn't meet one in Drake."

"I thought we agreed."

"I'm sorry, K. I couldn't resist." She snickered.

"Besides, I don't meet men like you do."

"Girl, I love you like a sister, but for the life of me I can't understand why you don't realize the spell you cast on men. K, you are gorgeous. With that good hair, flawless skin, light eyes, a model's figure, and a sister's butt, you are just what the doctor ordered. Add in that innocence and naivety you project and you are quite mysterious and desirable to most men."

"Really?"

"Yes, really."

"Innocence I project?" I asked, confused. "What are you talking about?"

"Yes, I don't know any twenty-eight-year-old woman who doesn't cuss, drink, or kiss on the first date."

"Taylor, stop exaggerating. I curse when I'm in rush-hour traffic and I do drink when we go out."

"Yeah, and when you do cuss, it sounds ridiculous. Who cusses using proper English? And two drinks is not what I call drinking."

We both laughed. It was the first laugh I'd had in a while and it felt good. Real good. I had forgotten the feeling.

"But, I love you anyway," Taylor offered.

"Love you back."

There was a moment of silence.

"I have to ask. Have you heard from him?"

"Who?"

"Girl, you know who. Don't act dumb. This is Taylor you're talking to."

"Drake?" I asked with some difficulty.

"Yes. Drake. Who else would I be talking about? I know by now he has tried to crawl back to you like the snake he is, by way of an apology or intimidation."

"Haven't heard from him. He knows it's over; we both realize that this time around."

"If you say so, K. I'll have to see it before I will believe it. It's still early in the breakup. I've seen y'all go through this break-up, get-back-together cycle numerous times. I realize you love him, but you are like some sort of trophy to Drake the way he is always showing you off. Wanting you to dress sexy. Wear your hair a certain way. He wants you to be someone you're not. Can't you see that? By the way, you never told me what the big breakup was all about? You guys have broken up so many times, I've lost count. What was it this time?"

"It doesn't even matter. I couldn't handle any more of his foul ways and this was definitely the end."

"It's amazing, a man that gorgeous with all those damn issues."

"Issues?"

"Yes, issues, girl. He has you so dick whipped that you can't see whether you are coming or going. Why the man make you dress up in costumes all the damn time? It ain't Halloween. Or the time he wouldn't let you touch him, and he sucked your tatas all night long? Girl, that was a trip when you told me about that. His breastfeeding days are long gone. You ain't his mama. What was up with that? Strange, I tell you."

I didn't say anything. I couldn't defend him. Taylor had seen Drake in action, more than once, and I had told her things about our relationship to determine if Drake's actions were normal.

"You are definitely going to the club with me, right?"

"I don't know. I'll let you know later in the week."

"K?" Taylor asked, irritated.

"I promise."

"Okay, cool. I guess I'll have to hold you to that. At least you didn't say no."

I heard a beep, indicating that I had another call on my other line. I figured it had to be for Mother. She had received more phone calls since she'd been staying with me than I typically received in a week.

"Hey, Taylor, hold on for a minute. I have another call."

"Okay, don't leave me holding, Kennedy. You know how I hate that shit."

"Girl, hold on."

I pushed the button to click over.

"Hello?"

"Hello, baby. How are you doing? I've missed you so much." I heard a deep, familiar, sexy voice, smooth as silk.

For a second, my heart fell down to my feet. My hands started to tremble uncontrollably. I don't even know how I managed to click back over to Taylor. I was functioning on autopilot after hearing the sound of his voice.

"Taylor, let me call you back. I have another call I need to take."

"Who is it?"

"Bye."

"It's him, isn't it?"

"Bye, girl. Quit being so nosey. I'll call you later."

"Kennedy, don't give in to him this time. Have a backbone. Please."

"Bye."

Slowly, I clicked back over and hugged my pillow closer.

"Hello?"

"Baby, what took you so long? I thought you had hung up on me. That would have hurt my heart."

"Taylor was on the other line."

"Probably talking about me."

"Drake, contrary to what you may think, we don't sit around discussing you all the time. The world doesn't revolve around you, believe it or not."

"Listen, baby, I didn't call to argue with you. Okay? Just talk to me," he stated, smooth as honey.

"What do you want, Drake?"

"I was just checking on you. I haven't seen you at work for a few days. Wanted to make sure you're okay. Besides, I miss you, baby."

"I'm fine. Is that all?" I asked coldly.

"Hold up. Listen, I want to see you, Kennedy."

"Can't. We are over. Remember?" I stated with no emotion.

"Baby, I could never stop loving you and we could never be over. Love doesn't cease to exist overnight."

"You never *started* loving me and we are definitely over. Believe that."

"Calm down. We can work this out, talk it out like always."

"Not this time."

"Just let me see you," Drake begged.

"See me? For what?"

"To bask in your beauty and make sweet love to you."

"You must be kidding. Have you forgotten what happened? Have you forgotten all those horrible things you said to me? Did to me? All the unspeakable names you called me?"

"Spoken in anger, that's all. I didn't mean any of it."

"Well, it hurt me just the same. Some things you can't take back."

There was a silence.

"Listen, I have to go. I can't do this," I whispered as tears threatened to spill forth.

"Baby, don't treat me like this. Don't treat *us* this way; give *us* another chance. We deserve that much."

"Me, what about you? You can never accept the blame for anything."

"Kennedy, calm down. You know how you get when you let your emotions get the best of you, and then you don't think rationally."

I didn't say anything. The double-talk was in full force.

"I love you. Seriously, we can work this out. I don't

want to lose you," he said in that sexy, deep voice. The voice I used to adore. Now, the one I despised with a passion.

"Too late. You already have. Lost me."

I actually heard my pitiful sobs before I realized I was crying. Fresh tears were spilling down my cheeks and I was totally surprised. I didn't think I had any more tears left for Drake. I didn't even have the strength to wipe them away as they fell onto my cover.

"Drake, don't do this to me," I managed to murmur between sobs.

"Sssh. Kennedy, I need to see you. I need to touch you, feel you. Fit snugly inside you, make you come."

"Don't, Drake. Let me go. You have to let me go."

"I can't do that, baby. Never. I need you too much. Need to feel you pressed up against me, underneath me. I yearn to cradle you in my arms, where you belong. Let me come over and I'll slowly lick my tongue over your clit, bury my tongue deep inside you, and make you feel good again. You don't have to do anything but lie there with your legs wide open for me."

"No."

"No?"

"That's what I said."

"Well, I'll be there in fifteen minutes. We'll discuss it while I'm undressing you."

"Don't, Drake. I have no desire to see you."

"Fifteen minutes."

"No. My mother is here."

"Damn, why didn't you tell me that before? When is she leaving?"

"She's not; I'm sick. Recovering from the flu. She's taking care of me."

"It figures. She treats you like you're a little girl; her precious baby."

"And you act like you're jealous of our mother-daughter relationship."

"Why would I be?"

"Because you can't have me one hundred percent."

"Kennedy, you're wrong. I already do."

"I'm hanging up."

"Tell me I'm wrong then."

Silence.

"I thought so."

"I need to go now," I stuttered.

"Anyway, we both know that you aren't Little Miss Innocent. Don't we? I think I'm one of the few people who has seen the real Kennedy Logan. The one you keep buried deep inside yourself. I've seen her come out and play and enjoy every inch."

"I have to go."

"What? Did I hit a nerve? The things I could tell Mommy Dearest."

"No, because I haven't done anything you didn't ask me to do. I did it all for love. For you."

"I bet you're creaming in your panties right now just thinking about us together. Me fucking you from behind."

"Drake, you are sick and you have nothing on me."

"Well, maybe if Mommy Dearest knew all the perverted acts her little princess has performed for me and on me, she'd think otherwise of your innocence."

"You make me sick. I can't stand your ass."

He continued, "Maybe if she knew how you can suck dick better than a pro."

Nothing but my cries were heard now; ones I didn't even recognize as my own. Deep, heart-wrenching sobs.

"Maybe if Mommy Dearest knew how much you love me to eat you out. You'd lie there for hours with your legs spread, if I let you. You love that shit."

Sobs. Loud cries.

"Or what about how I can get you to take it in the ass? Can't get many women to do that. Especially not a black woman."

"Why are you doing this to me? I haven't done anything to you but love you."

"And why are you crying? I told you, Kennedy, I was going to make you stronger; you're weak. Cry babies can't hang with the big boys. Get a backbone."

"Well, I won't hang with you. Don't call me again, Drake."

"You don't mean that, baby. You crave my touch. When can I see you again?"

"Never."

"I don't have to penetrate you. Just let me touch you. Like I used to."

"Leave me alone, I cried out loudly.

"See what I mean, Kennedy? Hang up on me. Scream, do something other than cry. Every time we argue, you cry. Your mom, your exes, Taylor, everybody pampers you. You need to toughen up, girl."

I didn't respond.

"Kennedy? Kennedy? Answer me, dammit. You will talk to me sooner or later. I guarantee it."

"I hate you. You hear me? I despise you. I regret the day I met you."

I didn't even attempt to hide my muffled cries from him.

"Is that why you did what you did?"

"I hate your lying ass so much," I screamed between sobs. "Stop twisting your perverted actions."

"I bet you'd do it again—for me. I go to sleep at night with images of that night flashing in my mind."

"Sweetie? Who are you talking to? What's wrong?" I heard Mother ask as she walked quickly up the hallway and into my bedroom to find me simply crying and holding the phone receiver away from my ear as if that would make Drake magically go away. Disappear.

"Hello? Hello? Who is this?" Mother asked.

"Hello, Mrs. Logan. How are you? I don't know what I said that upset Kennedy so badly. You know how fragile she is."

"Listen, Mr. Collins. I am not going to repeat this twice. I don't know who you think you are messing with, but I'm not Kennedy. Don't call over here upsetting my daughter again. Is that understood . . . What?"

I could hear Drake through the phone. "I said she can't hide from me forever. Tell her that."

"I'm ending this call in two seconds."

"She can't hide under your apron forever like she has milk on her tongue. Hand the phone back to—"

"One, two. Your two seconds are up."

Chapter 8

"Rise and shine, Kennedy. Rise and shine. Today is going to be a wonderful, beautiful day. Too gorgeous to sleep away like you did yesterday. Get up."

"Mother. I'm still sleepy."

"No, you aren't. You just think you're tired. Get up and get dressed, Kennedy," she exclaimed, tossing my covers to the floor. "Get up. Now."

I turned over so that I could look at her out of the corner of my eye. She was serious. Mother wasn't playing around this morning.

"Okay. Give me five minutes, Mother," I said, burying my head under the pillow.

"Five minutes is all you get, not a second longer. I'll see you at the breakfast table," she said, turning and walking out the door without another word or backward glance.

True to my word, a few minutes later I was seated at the breakfast table in my powder blue robe and gown. My hair was all over the place, and I didn't even bother to brush my teeth or wash my face. I still had crust on my face next to my mouth. I felt the way I looked. I didn't feel like doing anything, not even practicing good hygiene. If I had done what I usually do, and gotten cleaned up first, I would have been trying, once again, to please someone else.

Breakfast, which again consisted of scrambled eggs, bacon, and grits, smelled wonderful, but I didn't have an appetite. All I desired was sleep because I knew inner peace wasn't attainable. With sleep, I could forget for precious minutes.

After pouring freshly squeezed orange juice into our glasses, Mother fixed our plates and sat down in front of me. Then, out of the blue she started questioning me like a prosecuting attorney.

"Sweetie, what's going on?"

"What do you mean?" I asked, not bothering to look up, and playing the role of clueless brilliantly.

"Sweetie, you know what and who I'm talking about."

"Nothing. Nothing's going on," I said, glancing down again at my untouched plate. I couldn't meet Mother's eyes. I didn't want her to see the pain inside that crippled me on a daily basis.

"No, quite a lot is going on and I'm not about to close my eyes and pretend any longer that it isn't. Sooner or later, we need to discuss that, er, night."

"I don't want to talk about it," I whispered, feeling panic set in. I wanted to flee to my bedroom and to the protection of my covers. Talking about that night brought back unpleasant and dark memories that reminded me of another dark night.

"And you don't have to until you are ready. Sweetie, I care about you so much. Can't you see that? I don't want to see you in pain anymore because I can't stand to see you suffering. When you hurt, I hurt. I feel your pain."

"I'm not hurting." That statement wasn't a lie. All my

hurt and pain had been pushed back into a safe spot. Right now, I felt nothing. I was numb. I was empty. Simply existing. That's all I could muster the strength to do.

"I love you and know you like the back of my hand and I know when you are suffering. I have been there for every cut, scrape, and broken bone."

"Mother, please, I don't want to talk about this."

"I'm sorry, but we need to discuss this."

We stared at each other. I looked down first.

"I wanna know, what hold does Drake have on you? I thought you had broken it off with him."

"I did. We did."

"Why were you even talking with him the other night and crying your heart out?"

"Mother, just because we broke up doesn't mean I can't talk with the man ever again."

"Well, you shouldn't when he has you in hysterics. What did he say to you?"

"Nothing," I said, pushing eggs around on my plate and taking a bite of my crispy bacon.

"Kennedy? I'm not stupid."

"Nothing, Mother. Drake didn't say anything."

"Huh. It didn't sound like that to me. I never did like that arrogant, self-centered piece of a man. There's just something about him that I can't quite put my finger on, but I do know I can't stand his ass. I'm very perceptive and he's evil. Plain evil I tell you."

As I swallowed my grits and played some more with my eggs, I shrugged my shoulders and looked down at my almost full plate.

"Kennedy, I realize your daddy and I sheltered you when you were growing up. I know you haven't experienced a lot of serious relationships, but the way Drake treats you is wrong. Dead wrong, sweetie. You deserve better."

"Mother, I understand that. That's why we are not together," I stated calmly and matter-of-factly.

"Now, I realize you are sitting there acting like I'm the one who has lost my mind, but I also know how distraught you were the other night, and I didn't like what I saw. Not one bit."

"I was tired and I got overemotional. I let Drake's comments about how much he misses me get to me."

"Sweetie, it was more than that. After the, er, incident happened, you were calling out his name in your sleep, during the night at the hospital."

"Was I?"

"Yes. You were."

"Well, it didn't mean anything. We were once very close. I loved him," I said, staring at the far wall and praying that tears wouldn't spill forth.

"Kennedy, look at me. I'm only going to ask you this once. Did Drake have anything, anything at all to do with your, er, this situation? The note you left that night was pretty vague."

"No."

"Are you sure?"

"Absolutely, Mother." Lying was becoming easier and easier.

"Promise me you won't let that man upset you again. You don't have to talk to him again. Ever. He's not good for you. Not at all. Find yourself a nice, decent young man. There are plenty of good men in church."

"I'm not looking for a man."

"Well, promise me right now that you won't speak with Drake again."

"I won't speak with him again," I answered, realizing I was probably delivering an empty promise. However, for the moment, Mother looked pacified.

"Sweetie, you know what your daddy and I went through a few years ago, and I was devastated. But you cry, you scream, you throw stuff, say a few choice curse words, and then you get over it. You love yourself . . . and life goes on."

"I know. I know all that." Secretly, I thought, *sometimes it's not that simple. Everybody is not that strong. You can't love someone one day and the next day turn off all feelings. Life doesn't work like that. Love doesn't work like that. My love doesn't, anyway.*

"Okay, you've played with that food long enough. Kennedy, eat your breakfast before it gets cold. It probably already is. Do you want me to microwave it for you?" she asked.

"No. I'm fine, Mother."

"You sure?"

"Yes, I'm positive."

"Kennedy, we will work our way through all this mess. I pray for you each and every day," Mother whispered, reaching for my hand across the table. She gently squeezed and I squeezed back, thinking how my life would never be the same.

After breakfast, I decided to sit out on my wide, wooden deck for a change of pace. It wasn't too cool; more like sweater weather. The neighborhood was quiet and peaceful. Most people had returned to work after the holidays and their routines resumed to normal. The only sounds were of squirrels scampering around in the dry leaves that lined the ground. Mother had fixed some hot mint tea and I reclined in one of my patio chairs, wrapped in a throw, and sipped it. I found myself in a reflective mode, so I decided to retrieve my journal and write for a while. Mother's words had effectively reached me.

Dear Journal,

I was a coward yet again. I allowed Drake to penetrate me emotionally, and I didn't bother to stand up for myself. Again. It seems he always knows exactly what buttons to push. I now know what a love-hate relationship feels like. I hate Drake so much that I can almost taste the loathing dripping off me like sweat. Yet, there is a small part of me, shoved way back there, that will always love him. Our relationship wasn't always so toxic and painful. We didn't always mix like oil and water. Not at all. Actually, things started out like a sweet dream that I wanted to replay over and over again. Why does love always turn sour?

Approximately a week after I was introduced to Drake at work, I picked up my ringing phone to find him on line two.

"Miss Logan?"

"Yes, speaking."

"This is Drake Collins."

"Hi. How are you?"

"Good, and yourself?"

"I'm great. How are you adjusting to the company and your new role?"

"I can't complain. Everything is going well both on and off the job. Everyone I've met in Atlanta has extended true Southern hospitality. Strang-

ers actually speak to you in the streets and look you in the eyes, and everyone is super friendly and laid back. I really think I'm going to enjoy living here."

"That's good."

"Listen, I don't know what your schedule looks like today, but would you have a few minutes, maybe an hour, to walk me through some of these reports? I know you service most of the clients on this list."

I looked around at the pile of paperwork on my desk, but found myself agreeing to come up to his office in twenty minutes.

"Sure, I can squeeze you in."

"It won't be a problem?" Drake questioned in that deep voice that I loved to hear.

"No, not at all. See you in twenty."

"Great. You're a sweetheart, Miss Logan. I owe you one."

Exactly twenty minutes later, after making a quick trip to the restroom, brushing my teeth, and combing through my thick mane of hair, I was softly knocking at Mr. Collins's closed door.

"Come in."

I slowly opened the door and strolled in. Drake was working with an Excel spreadsheet on his PC. He looked up and smiled in my direction. Perfect white teeth. Again, I couldn't get over how utterly gorgeous he was. I simply stared. And he was all man. Solid. Drake carried himself like a man definitely in charge of any situation. I admired that.

"Hi, Kennedy. You're right on time," he stated, looking down at his gold wristwatch.

I still stood near the open door.

"Come on in, and close the door because it's been pretty hectic and noisy on the floor today. I don't want us to be disturbed."

"Okay. Sure." I shut the door and was enveloped into his space.

Standing up, he said, "You can take my chair. I'm going to be walking back and forth and pulling files, et cetera. It'll be easier for you to sit and for me to stand."

"Sounds like a plan."

I took a seat in his black, soft leather swivel chair and felt his alluring fragrance and aura completely overtake me. As I made myself comfortable, Drake pulled out a stack of computer printouts and laid them in the center of his elegant cherrywood desk, and deposited himself on the edge of the desk, right next to me. With his suit jacket off and the sleeves to his white starched shirt rolled up, it was obvious that Drake was ready to get down to some serious business.

"Miss Kennedy, what is this mess? I can't make heads or tails out of most of it. There are all these acronyms for everything. Where is a list that explains all the codes?"

I picked up a stack of the paperwork that he was referring to, reviewed them briefly, and started to explain what we were looking at in reference to our clients, their demographics, bundles, etc. The entire time, I was very aware of Drake being very near. So close. I could feel the heat rising from his body. I could see the tiny hairs standing up on his arms. Too close for comfort. Definitely.

When he was reviewing the printouts, I used that time to secretly check him out closer. He had the smoothest brown skin and his hands were so large, yet smooth. His haircut was perfect, like he had just stepped out of a barber's chair, and the way his eyelashes swooshed over his eyelids was super sexy.

At one point, he stopped looking at the printouts and glanced over at me. For a moment, I thought he had caught me staring. I panicked. Coughing, I quickly looked down at the report in front of me.

"What is that enticing perfume you're wearing? It smells wonderful."

"Ellen Tracy."

"Smells nice on you," he said, and went back to examining the trail of paperwork he had laid out in neat stacks on his desk and credenza.

"Thank you."

A couple of times I thought I felt him staring down my low-cut silk blouse that I wore with a straight black skirt and black pumps. From Drake's point of view, he could clearly see my black lace bra and probably could see the swell of my breasts as they rose and fell in his presence with a desire and mind of their own.

"Where is that list of codes?" Drake asked, looking around at the stacks of paperwork on his desk.

"There they are, third stack from your right," I explained as we both reached for the code sheet at the same time. When his hand touched my fingers, I experienced cool chills running up and down my arms. I quickly placed my hands back in my lap to steady them.

"Good. This is exactly what I need. Thank you."

"You're welcome."

Running his hand across his head, Drake absently glanced down at his wristwatch.

"You know what? I've kept you long enough today. I didn't realize it was so late and you haven't even eaten lunch."

"No, but I'm glad to help out any way I can."

"Miss Logan, you've been an incredible help. Unfortunately, we only made it through a quarter of the reports. Can we meet again next week? Say, next Friday at ten o'clock?" he asked, looking at me expectantly. "Is that asking too much?"

"No. That shouldn't be a problem."

"How about scheduling two hours on your calendar?"

"I'll see what I can do."

"If you'd like, I can check with your manager to make sure she's cool with it. Your manager is Peggy Hunt, isn't she?"

"Yes."

"Good. That'll give me the chance to put in a good word for you as well. Let her know what a great asset you've been."

"You don't have to do that."

"I know, but I want to," Drake volunteered, with that smile shining bright.

"Thanks, that'll be wonderful."

"Okay, then, next week it is. Take care, Miss Logan."

"You too," I said, retrieving my belongings, then opening the door and heading out with a warm tingling coursing between my legs.

Wednesday of the following week I ran into Drake in the lobby, down by the security desk. He was talking with someone who I recalled meeting at an interdepartmental business meeting, one of the senior managers. Drake abruptly ended their conversation, came up behind me, and fell in pace. The fluttering began again.

"Hi, Miss Logan." He smiled. I adored that smile.

"Hi, Mr. Collins." I grinned back, looking up at him. He was so tall.

"Please, call me Drake."

"Well, in that case, please call me Kennedy." We grinned at each other again.

"Where are you headed?"

I held up my lunch bag. "Since the women on my floor are seriously tripping today, I decided to sit in the cafeteria with my leftovers from last night and read."

Drake reached to check out the cover of the book I held in my other hand. "Is it good?"

"So far it's excellent, pulls the reader in right from the very beginning. It's by a local Atlanta author."

"I'm headed to lunch too, but I hate eating alone. Could you join me?"

"I don't know. I was—"

"I'll even buy. Come on, say yes. I owe you for all your hard work last week."

"Really, it's not necessary. I was just doing my job."

"I'm not taking no for an answer," he stated, looking at me like he wasn't going anywhere until I said yes.

"Okay, sure. Since you put it that way, why not?" I said as I left my lunch bag at the security desk for safekeeping.

"Where would you like to eat, Kennedy?"

"I've overheard my coworkers talking about this recently opened Italian restaurant that's within walking distance and has delicious lunch specials."

"Excellent. Lead the way," he said, opening the door that led to the busy street.

As we walked the couple of blocks, I noticed women checking Drake out. He walked with a confident stride and air about himself; he had swagger.

An hour later, an hour that flew by, I couldn't believe I had laughed, talked, and had such a wonderful time. The food was mouthwatering and the conversation even better. Our conversation wasn't forced; it came natural and easy. As I ate my seafood pasta and Greek salad, Drake had me in stitches over some of his tales of growing up in Los Angeles. His descriptions were so vivid, I felt like I was right there with him.

I found myself opening up in ways I never expected. I surprised myself by confiding in him about my dissatisfaction with my current position. He seemed to genuinely understand and even offered suggestions and advice. A few times I would glance up and find him staring at me. I'd look down and play with a strand of my hair in order to avoid his eyes, which appeared to reach within my soul and seek out my deepest desires.

"May I ask you a personal question?" he asked, suddenly serious.

"Sure, why not? Ask away."

"Are you seeing or dating anyone in particular?"

I paused for only a moment. "No and no."

"That's hard to believe. A beautiful lady like yourself, I would think you'd have men beating down your front door every night."

"I'm afraid not," I said, twirling another strand of my hair around and through my middle fingers.

"Why is that?"

"I'm afraid I'm too picky and selective."

"What are you saying? There aren't any good men in Atlanta?"

"If there are, I'm not meeting them."

"Is it true that there's a large and growing gay and lesbian population?"

"That's what I've been told. Atlanta isn't called the new San Francisco for no reason."

"Interesting. You know, you remind me so much of my first love. She was kinda quiet, with your smoldering, alluring beauty and innocent sexiness."

I blushed. "Really?" I asked, breaking our eye contact.

"I'm sorry, I shouldn't have said that. That was inappropriate. I apologize if I made you uncomfortable in any way."

"No, I'm fine."

Drake glanced down at his watch. "Man, look at the time. I guess we'd better be getting back before they come looking for us and while we still have jobs." He signaled for the waiter and the check.

"You're right, my manager demands promptness from our team. I wouldn't want to get on her black list because of tardiness."

He winked conspiratorially. "Don't worry. I'll handle her. If she asks, I'll say we were on a boring business lunch that dragged on."

Drake and I made it back to the building and waited at the first bank of elevators to go up to our floors. The elevator doors opened and a stream of people rushed out. As we stepped in, surprisingly, he and I were the only two people in the elevator. I stood to one side and Drake stood on the other. There was a comfortable silence that only we could truly appreciate.

"Drake, thanks for the lunch. I see what I'm missing by eating at my desk all the time. I seriously have to go out more and enjoy the Midtown restaurants."

"I definitely enjoyed the meal and the company. See you Friday, Kennedy," he said as we arrived at my floor and I stepped off. "Kennedy?" he called, pushing the button to keep the elevator door open.

"Yes?" I stopped walking and turned around.

"Don't worry. You'll meet that special man soon."

"If you say so."

"Trust me." The door shut with me still starring at it and trying to figure out his hidden message.

On Friday, I was back in Drake's office, behind closed doors again. Since Fridays were casual, I was dressed down in a cotton, long-sleeve button-down shirt and dark navy blue slacks with my hair pulled back in a ponytail. I was looking more like a college student than a professional businesswoman. But at least I didn't overdo it,

like some of the women on my floor who obviously
thought Casual Friday meant Nightclub Friday.

Drake had on a tennis shirt embossed with our
corporate logo, and khaki pants. Even dressed
down, the man was all that. Now that I had gotten
a better view of those abs, I had an overwhelming urge to reach out and squeeze them. I couldn't
deny it—the man was making me crazy.

"Let me get up so you can claim your seat," he
laughed, showing those straight white teeth that
reminded me of the sexy actor Taye Diggs.

I smiled, somewhat shyly. "Thank you, sir. Good
afternoon."

"Oh, let's not go back to that formality. We had
a great lunch the other day and I thought all those
barriers came down with the meal. Deal?"

"Deal."

As I moved into my assigned seat, we briefly
brushed against each other and my nipples instantly hardened like he had stroked them. Drake
smelled divine.

"Excuse me," I said, catching my breath.

"Sure. You look nice today, but you always look
good."

"Thanks. Are you ready to get started?"

"First, I want to ask you something."

"Okay." I looked up at him expectantly, waiting
for his question.

"This is totally not business related, but I feel
comfortable around you. I hope you feel the same
about me."

I stared at him and searched his face, unsure of
what he was going to ask me. I guess Drake saw
uncertainty reflected in my eyes.

"Really, my question is nothing major. I went to a nightclub the other night and almost got mobbed by the women there. Are Atlanta women always that aggressive?"

I laughed and exhaled. "I don't know, I guess so from what I've heard. I don't do the club scene much, but the women in Atlanta are pretty bold. The women-to-men ratio is pretty high, so the competition is fierce and no holds barred."

"I see. Well, curious minds wanted to know. That's all. It's cool. I had women asking me to dance, wanting to buy me drinks and take me home."

"Welcome to Atlanta."

He didn't say anything, just stared at me.

"What?"

"Nothing. I probably shouldn't say this again, but you are a beautiful woman, Kennedy."

"And thank you again," I said, looking off before Drake saw how flustered he was making me.

"No, really, you are gorgeous. Are my comments making you uncomfortable?" he asked, searching my face for answers.

"Of course not. I love being told I'm beautiful by a handsome man," I said, laughing my nervous giggle. I found myself searching for strands of my hair to twist between my fingers. I forgot it was up in a ponytail. So my hand hung in the air, making me feel foolish.

"You should be used to it by now, Kennedy." Drake's eyes never left my face. Was he searching for a reaction?

There was an awkward, uncomfortable silence

as I felt my face heat up. In my nervousness, I shuffled the paperwork on his desktop.

"Well, I guess we need to get to work and earn our paychecks. I only have two of your precious hours and we still have a lot to cover."

"Let's dig in," I stated, eager to get back to business-related matters. I was more comfortable discussing clients and their needs.

Drake and I worked steadily for over an hour. I typed codes into his Excel spreadsheet and my neck was getting stiff, so I found myself massaging it with my free hand. Without expecting it, Drake came up behind me.

"Got a kink?"

I nodded and kept typing.

"Here, let me fix that." Drake proceeded to firmly but gently knead the muscles of my neck with his large hands. It felt so good that I found myself closing my eyes and reclining against his expert hands.

"How's that? Better?"

"Much better." I didn't want him to stop.

"Good," he said as his hand inched further down. I could feel the heat of his fingertips through my thin cotton shirt. He hesitated.

I froze too, stiff as a board. I didn't breathe. Didn't dare to.

"Kennedy, I know this sounds crazy, but I have this overwhelming urge to touch you."

I didn't say anything. I didn't know what to say, or do, because this man was my superior. With my back to him, I kept staring at the computer screen like it held all the answers. The secret to life. My mind was screaming, Yes, yes, yes, touch me, but my tongue wouldn't verbalize it.

I was in conflict because I would be going against my self-imposed work policy about dating coworkers. Or would this be considered sexual harassment. Yet, I'd never had such a strong sexual attraction to any man before. Drake was the complete package: handsome, professional, financially secure, well-rounded, and sexy. Drake had it all; he was every woman's dream. Even Mother would approve.

"Kennedy?" Drake asked, pressing his hand against my shoulder.

I didn't say anything. I couldn't. By now, my chest was heaving up and down. My mind was screaming for me to stop this madness before it went too far. However, I wasn't thinking with my brain.

"Kennedy?" Every time Drake spoke my name, his right hand went down a little further. Almost there.

"Kennedy, talk to me, Do you want this?" This time his hand made contact. I tensed up and immediately found myself relaxing as his fingers skillfully began caressing my breasts and hard, throbbing nipples. Without realizing it, I leaned into his hand and embraced his touch.

"Hmmm. You feel so good. Just like I imagined. I dreamed about you the other night." His fingers were kneading firmly, but gently. When he tweaked my nipple between his thumb and forefinger, I swooned.

"Turn around, let me see you." He proceeded to swirl my chair around and I was flushed. I looked down at the floor.

He slowly, gently lifted my chin back up. "Look at me." His eyes never left mine as he proceeded to unbutton the tiny buttons on my shirt. He took his time, drawing out the anticipation.

I was breathing so deeply I thought I would hyperventilate and need a brown paper bag to breathe into.

"Drake, I'm not sure about this."

"Sssh, it's okay," he softly whispered, rubbing his index finger sensually across my lips. It was so light; it felt like being touched by a feather.

"Somebody might walk in."

"Kennedy, take a chance. Trust me. My associates know not to disturb me when my door is closed. Beautiful," he said, proceeding to lift up my lacy bra and push it out of the way. My breasts were fully exposed, sitting high, and my nipples were already proudly erect. On display. Beckoning him. Welcoming him.

There wasn't any more talking. Drake bent down in front of me, without my permission, and proceeded to suck my breasts like a starving man. He was definitely a breast man because this went on for about thirty minutes with him sucking, touching, licking, and squeezing them until I moaned out loud several times. Perfect care was given to each breast.

Drake made me feel so good. I held on to the side of my chair and gave into the wonderful sensations as he pulled me near. The only sounds were our breathing, moaning, and his sucking. My nipples were as hard as they had ever been, and every time he tweaked them, I moaned out loud.

He didn't touch me anywhere else. Drake didn't even kiss my lips, only my neck. He showered me with light, delicate kisses, whispered in my ear, and sucked my breasts some more, tenderly biting down on my nipples. He was on a mission. Finally, he stopped abruptly and stood back up. I couldn't read the blank expression on his face.

"Kennedy, you're a sweet lady. So sweet," he stated, gently cupping my face.

I didn't respond. I couldn't. He had taken my breath away.

Drake leaned back down and stroked my nipples between his fingers one more time. Had a nipple in each hand, pulling. Again, an involuntary moan of pleasure escaped me as I saw a small smile of victory grace his face.

"That should take the edge off," he said with a sparkle in his eyes. "Listen, why don't we knock off for today. We've accomplished a lot, but let's meet again next week."

"I don't know," I said, swiftly and awkwardly buttoning up my shirt.

"I've already talked with your manager and she said I could have you as long as I need you."

"Did she?" I questioned.

"So it's settled. Same time next week," Drake said, sitting on the edge of his desk and intensely watching me as I clumsily fastened the last button on my shirt. My breasts were straining to be free again. To be handled by him. Same time then."

"Sure."

"How you feeling?" he asked, teasing my breasts through the fabric of my blouse and making me light-headed.

"Okay."

"Just okay? Well, I haven't done my job effectively."

"I'm feeling great," I volunteered too eagerly.

"That sounds better. Much better."

Drake was still caressing, probing, feeling me up.

"Well, I'd better go." I stood on weak knees.

"Are you sure?" he asked, towering over me, still touching me. His hand was underneath my shirt; squeezing, fondling, tweaking.

"I'd better get back. I only allocated two hours for this project." I barely managed to get the words out.

Drake had sat back on the edge of his desk and he stared at me with lust-filled eyes as he gently pulled me to him, within his open legs. I clearly saw the outline of his hard, thick dick. He caught me looking and grinned. I quickly looked away, feeling like I'd been caught by the teacher doing something bad.

Pressing my hand against his erection, he lowered his head and bit down on each nipple through my shirt, then stated, "If you're sure."

"I'm sure," I managed to mutter. "I have to go." A lump had formed in my throat.

Palming my butt cheeks and pulling me into him, he said, "You have pretty breasts."

"I really have to go."

"Take care then," he said, pulling down and smoothing out my shirt.

I proceeded to gather my pen, purse, and other belongings. I was totally confused as to what *had just happened. I knew what had occurred, but Drake was now acting like nothing was out of the ordinary. He was seated at his desk and writing something on a Post-it note, oblivious to my departure.*

"See you next week," I said, for lack of anything better to say. My trembling hand was on the doorknob.

"And Kennedy?" he stated right before I opened the door. He didn't even look up.

"Yes?"

"Next Friday, wear a skirt."

Chapter 9

"Hello. Daddy, what a pleasant surprise," I squealed into the phone. Mother sat across from me on the sofa and pretended to watch *Wheel of Fortune*. I saw her ears perk up at the mention of her ex-husband. Most of the time she pretended like he didn't exist. Sometimes pretending keeps you sane.

"How ya doing, baby girl?" Daddy asked in that deep Southern drawl that I loved.

Daddy was a true Southern gentleman in every aspect of the word. He was the type of man who opened doors for his woman, pulled out her chair at a restaurant, who stood up when she entered a room, who held his woman's hand, who sent her roses or left "just because" notes under her pillow. Daddy did all that and more when he was married to Mother. That's why after thirty-plus years of marriage, everyone was shocked when Daddy, at the ripe old age of sixty, up and left Mother for a younger woman and moved down to Florida. At the time, I thought Mother was going to have a nervous breakdown. She refused to accept it. That was five years ago.

"I'm doing okay, Daddy." Mother and I had decided not to tell Daddy about my, er, situation. There was no reason to worry and upset him too.

"How's work?"

"Work is fine. How is Loretta?" I asked out of courtesy more than anything else. Loretta was his lady friend. Out of the corner of my eye, I saw Mother cringe at the mere mention of that woman's name. Mother detested the ground she walked on and the air she breathed.

"Fine. Fine."

"Good."

"You've got to come down and visit us this summer. Have a little sun and fun. Relax and see your old man."

"I'll see what I can work out."

"Baby girl, you say that every year and you haven't made it yet."

"Maybe this year will be different. You never know." Secretly, I really did want to see him, but I knew Mother would take it as an act of betrayal. She claimed she couldn't stand the thought of him, but I knew she'd reconcile in a minute if he sought it. As for now, she thought Daddy was an old fool for abandoning his family the way he did. I tried to remain neutral, because I loved them both and didn't want to be forced to choose sides.

"I hope so. I miss you and I can't travel like I used to when I was a young man. I wanna see you before I kick the bucket."

"Daddy."

"Well, it's true. I'm not getting any younger. We all have to meet our maker someday; we can't live forever."

"Well, you can," I joked. He laughed that hearty chuckle that I adored so much.

"You still dating that young man you told me about? What was his name, David or something like that?"

"Drake?"

"Yeah, that's it."

My body instantly tensed and my stomach muscles knotted up. "No, I'm no longer dating him. We broke up."

"Hmm. I see. Well, maybe you can kiss and make up, because I'd love to have some grandchildren before I leave this earth. Just two or three who look like their precious mom."

"Daddy, as I said, you are going to be around for a long time to come. You haven't been sick a day in your life; Mother used to always say you are healthy as a horse. And there's no fixing this between me and Drake."

"Well, baby girl, you know best. Follow your heart. Sometimes you just have to go your separate ways. If it wasn't meant to be, it wasn't meant to be. Just follow your heart and it won't steer you wrong."

"You're right," I murmured more to myself than to Daddy.

"What's old gal been up to lately?" I discreetly held my hand over my mouth to keep from laughing out loud.

"Who?" I asked, knowing full well who he was referring to.

"You know who, your mother, Dorothy."

"Oh, nothing much. She's doing great."

"Yeah, I bet, butting into everybody's business. That didn't change overnight." He grunted.

I smiled and glanced over at Mother who wanted me to believe that she was all into *Wheel of Fortune*. I knew she was clinging to every word I spoke, trying to decipher what was being said on the other end of the phone by Daddy.

"Well, baby girl, I'm not going to hold you. I just

wanted to say hello and tell you that I love you, and I miss you. If you need anything, any money, anything at all, just call. And, baby girl, you know you can pick up the phone and call me sometimes too. I love speaking with you. Remember that, I'm just a phone call away."

"Okay, Daddy, I know and I will. I love you too."

"Well, you don't act like it. It's been five years since I left and I'm very happy with Loretta, but I divorced your mother, not you. One day you'll learn that sometimes you have to live for the moment and not worry about what people will think of you, because the future is not always promised."

"I understand—"

"No, hear me out now. That was your mother's problem. She was always worried about keeping up with the Joneses, or what someone would think about her if she did this, or didn't do that. Don't live your life that way. The only radical thing she ever did was to marry me without her parents' blessing."

I didn't say anything. Daddy was on a roll. When he went into one of these rare tirades all you could do was hear him out.

"Baby girl, happiness isn't promised. Sometimes you have to seek it and work hard to keep it, but one thing I've learned in all my years here on this earth: *if you don't love yourself, then don't expect anyone else to either.*"

"Daddy, you don't have to explain this to me. You don't need to justify your actions to me. I respect your decision."

"Well, I wish Dorothy did. I've tried calling her over the years and she always hangs up after a few unpleasant choice words I can't repeat."

"Well, don't take it to heart."

"Yeah, you're probably right. Like I said before, that woman will never change. Her entire stuck-up family has always held onto a grudge like it was their last dollar and ten cents. They never thought I was good enough for her and your mother was always stubborn as a mule."

I chose not to comment. I felt funny talking with Daddy about Mother with her sitting less than a foot away from me. I played with a strand of my hair with my free hand.

"Listen to me go on and on. Let me let you go. I'll talk to you soon, baby."

"Daddy. Take care of yourself and I love you."

"Me too. Bye now."

Before I could even put down the receiver, Mother came at me with fifty questions. "What did that fool want? He still shacking up? What did he say about me?"

"What fool?" I teased.

"Child, you know who I'm talking about. Don't act like you slow."

"Daddy?"

"Yes, that fool."

"Oh nothing, Daddy was just calling to say hello," I said, pretending to get lost in the game show.

"Ummph. Did he say anything about me?"

"He asked how you were doing."

"Ummph. Next time, tell him not to worry about me. He'd better worry about that forty-five-year-old hussy and home wrecker he's living with in sin."

I didn't open my mouth to utter one word. I simply stared at the TV screen and pretended to attempt to solve the next puzzle on *Wheel of Fortune*. A proper noun. I didn't want to get Mother started. Daddy was

Mother's first real boyfriend, first love, first everything, and they married shortly after she graduated from Morris Brown College in Atlanta.

Prior to retiring, Mother worked as a librarian for DeKalb County, and Daddy worked as a mechanic for Metro Atlanta Rapid Transit Authority (MARTA). You would have thought their love was everlasting the way Mother doted on Daddy, and the way he appeared to adore her. Even when doctors determined that Mother couldn't have children due to an injury she had suffered as a child, Daddy hung in there and assured her of his undying love, and a few years later they adopted me. From outside appearances they were living a blessed and loving life.

I don't understand what happened. Maybe it was a late, very late, midlife crisis that led Daddy to start up with Loretta and leave Mother for her. Who knows? Mother and I never saw it coming. It was so out of character for Daddy. He gave up everything for this other woman. Was she worth it? All I know is, when I spoke with Daddy he appeared happy.

Chapter 10

Now that Mother didn't have Daddy to dote on, I was next in line. So, here she sat on my sofa, munching on red seedless grapes, almost a month after my situation. Sometimes, the constant attention was overbearing, but I knew she meant well and was still worried about me. I had tried to persuade her to return to her own home, but Mother wasn't having that. She wasn't leaving until she knew for certain that I was fully recovered and wouldn't try anything so dangerous again.

I wanted my apartment back. I was a loner. I was used to being alone; I relished my own company. Except for when Drake used to visit or spend the night, or when Taylor stopped by for girlfriend talk, my apartment was my solitary haven. I longed to walk around in a short T-shirt, take long, hot baths, play my music, read my African American books, and light my scented candles. Sure, I could do that with Mother here, but it just wasn't the same.

I hadn't even gone back to work yet. Mother had convinced me to take some personal time by using vacation and unpaid days. I explained to my manager that I had a family emergency and no questions were asked. My employer was very family oriented. However, my time off had quickly slipped by and Monday I would return to work. Today was Saturday. Monday,

I would receive my real life back. Monday, I would see Drake for the first time in over a month.

I could honestly say that I wasn't going to try to take my life again. I had prayed about it and asked God for forgiveness and peace. I admit I was still depressed—that didn't just go away overnight but I realized I did have something to live for. I had a decent life before Drake and I'd survive after him.

The last few weeks, Mother had pretty much forced me to get up and dressed every single day. We had developed a routine. Some days we went to the park and walked. Other times we sat on the park bench and watched the stay-at-home moms play with their adorable, but active, children. Of course, through it all, she kept me well fed with delicious home-cooked meals and very pampered. In my weakest moments, I dreamt of what Drake and I could have had together. If only he had truly loved me.

One day, Mother and I took in a matinee and had an early dinner afterward at a popular seafood restaurant. A few days ago, we even dropped by the library and visited some of her old friends that Mother used to work with before she retired.

"It must be nice to be a lady of leisure, Dorothy," a gray-haired woman exclaimed. "You look wonderful. Retirement is definitely agreeing with you."

"Thank you. I try to stay busy and active," Mother said, leaning in for a big hug. "I saw some of the others up front. It's so good to see everybody."

"Same here. I'm so happy you dropped by."

"Betty, I would like you to meet my daughter, Kennedy."

"Well hi, Kennedy."

"Hello," I said.

"You are such a lovely girl, and I heard so much

about you when your mother and I worked together that I feel as if I know you."

I smiled.

"Let me tell you, your mother is so proud of you. When you went off to college that was all she talked about for weeks."

I blushed.

"Goodness, was I that bad?" Mother asked.

"No, no. We enjoyed hearing of Kennedy's adventures," Betty said.

"Well, I'm not going to stay long. Kennedy and I were in the area and I wanted to stop and say hello to everyone. I'll call you and maybe we can go out to lunch soon."

"That sounds good. You know the number, and my schedule, it hasn't changed."

"I'll do that," Mother stated.

"It was wonderful meeting you, Kennedy. I see now why your mother is so proud of you. You are a lovely young woman. Take care of her and yourself."

Some evenings, I would lay my head in her lap and Mother would comb and brush my hair like she did when I was a child. She'd hum a soft tune; I'd close my eyes and enjoy the sensation of the brush gently stroking my hair.

"I remember how you used to love for me to brush your hair when you were a child," Mother said. "You'd run to your room in your pj's and grab your special brush, sprint back into the living room, and lay your head in my lap, just like now. I would start with smooth, even, gentle strokes and would always have to brush at least one hundred times before I could stop. Sometimes you would fall asleep before I finished."

"I had a special brush?"

"You did. It had a gold-plated handle and you called it your princess brush."

"That's funny," I said, closing my eyes and enjoying the sensation of the strokes.

"Yeah, those were the days." Mother laughed, reminiscing about days gone by. "I think your daddy used to get a bit jealous because you never wanted him to brush your hair, only me."

She laughed and I took comfort in the memory.

One night, Mother and I gave each other manicures and pedicures. I could feel my spirit slowly mending and I knew without a doubt I was very loved.

"No, Mother, you have to trust me," I said, enjoying the moment.

"I don't want to wear pink fingernail polish, Kennedy."

"You've been wearing that skin-tone, tan polish for as long as I can remember. Try something different tonight. For me."

Mother slowly gave me her right hand.

"I trust you, sweetie. It's time for me to switch it up."

"Don't be scared," I kidded.

I laughed and proceeded to paint her nails hot pink.

"So, what do you think?" I asked as I finished and looked at my work.

"It's different. That's for sure."

I looked at her and saw the girl Daddy fell in love with; she was still there.

"I bet your gentleman friend will love this."

Mother blushed and surprised me by saying, "I bet he will. Do my toes."

To her credit, she wore it for a week before taking it off.

***

Most days, I didn't think of Drake. Other days, he's all I thought of; I even saw him in my dreams, when I closed my eyes at night. He hadn't attempted to call me, that I knew of, since the last time he had me in tears. Drake was right: he would see me sooner or later because we worked for the same company. In time, we would run into each other, and Drake was a very patient man. That I knew for a fact. The question was, would I be strong enough to see him?

Mother and I had already eaten; the dinner dishes were washed, dried, and placed back in the cabinets. It was a quiet, lazy Saturday evening and I decided to retire to my room and write in my journal. It was amazing how therapeutic writing my feelings and thoughts down was becoming. Seeing the details on paper put everything into clear focus. Some of my confessions were shameful, but I blamed them on love.

Mother wanted to ride out for ice cream later on. Her one vice was Baskin Robbins's butter pecan, two scoops. Of course, I knew tomorrow was church. She had forced me to attend church service for the last few Sundays. Mother said for me to hand my problems over to Jesus and He'd fix them. I truly hoped so because my problems were many and I couldn't handle them by myself. So I sought divine intervention.

As she dozed off, head bobbing now and then, I glanced over at Mother. Her reading glasses were perched on the tip of her nose and the newspaper she was reading had fallen, scattered, to the floor at her feet. She really was a great person, and I loved her for all she had done for me. She had put her life on hold for me.

I didn't want to hurt Mother, but I had made the decision to search for my birth mom and I intended to ask Taylor to help me with the process. It was a big step, but I needed to know where I came from; I felt it would help me in my recovery process to finally have my questions about my birth family answered. I felt that some of my insecurities, which hindered my relationships, were rooted in feelings of abandonment by my birth mother.

After her divorce, Mother gradually built a new life for herself. I was so proud of her. Now she had a male friend who took her places and treated her like a queen. She had one close girlfriend, Mrs. Baker, who visited and gossiped with her. Since her retirement last year, she was even more active in her social and civic organizations. Other than talking on the phone to them, she had given up these people and activities to care for me.

By now, Mother was in serious sleep mode and was softly snoring, even though she'd swear up and down that she didn't. As I bent down to kiss her cheek, I placed a dark green throw across her torso, then walked to my bedroom with a can of Coca-Cola in hand. Drake was always telling me I drank too much soda. In the past, when we went out, he would refuse to buy me any at restaurants. He made me drink water. For a while, I tried to heed his advice and totally cut them out, but now, I found myself drinking two or more each day.

I found my journal where I had last laid it down. Reading over the last entry was sort of painful. What was I thinking? What was I doing? Unfortunately, I wasn't thinking with my head and the situation only got worse. A lot worse.

Chapter 11

Dear Journal,

After what transpired in Drake's office, I should have run for the hills. I've never, ever done anything like that in my life. I can't believe I let it happen. Maybe it was the thrill and excitement of it all. Perhaps, it was doing things that were not in my character that made me give in to him. Maybe the fact that Drake was my superior had something to do with it, or was it that he brought out a sexuality in me I didn't even know existed?

To my credit, I will admit that during the preceding week, I debated back and forth whether I'd show up at the appointed time. To be honest, I could have easily gotten out of it by telling my manager that my workload was too heavy. I purposely avoided Drake by not venturing into our lobby area during lunch, not even to take care of personal matters. I literally camped out in my cubicle and hoped that he wouldn't call. Every time an internal call came through, I prayed it wasn't Drake.

I was totally confused over what had happened. My feelings flip-flopped back and forth. One minute I was flattered that he liked me, the next I wondered, did he really like me or did he think I was some sort of whore for what I let him do to me? One thing I was sure of, I was very attracted to Drake. Probably more attracted to him than any other man I had ever met. It didn't help that word had gotten out about him on my floor and my coworkers were constantly making comments about the sexy new manager upstairs and what he could do for them.

Basically for seven days my mind was in a total state of chaos. My emotions bounced back and forth like a tennis match. When Friday finally arrived, I still wasn't sure what my final decision would be. I had picked up the phone several times to cancel our meeting and make up some excuse as to why I needed to. However, there was just something about Drake that drew me to him. I couldn't stay away until I learned and experienced more.

At my designated time, I found myself taking the elevator up to his floor. As requested, I was dressed in a casual skirt and top. I don't know why Drake made that particular request, but I obliged him. As usual, I knocked on the closed door, and heard Drake's sexy voice requesting that I come in. I took two deep breaths, because it was now or never, and stepped into the office of the man who, in the months that followed, I would blindly love and follow.

"Hi." I smiled timidly. Being in Drake's presence brought out all my insecurities. I always wondered if I looked pretty enough or was intelligent enough. After all, he could have his pick of women. Why choose me?

"Hey, Kennedy. Give me a minute," he stated in

a direct, professional tone. He hadn't even looked up from his paperwork.

"Take your time." In my nervousness, I found myself playing with a strand of my hair and biting down on my bottom lip.

Drake, dressed in a pair of linen pants and button-down shirt, looked very serious today. There was no indication of what had gone down only a week earlier. This day, he was Mr. Professional. I was beginning to think that I'd imagined the entire incident; maybe it was an erotic dream.

Drake proceeded to pull out the final stack of reports and place it next to me on the desk. We were in our usual position: me sitting at his desk, in his chair, and Drake alternating between sitting on the edge of his desk or standing up behind me.

"Looks like we can finally see the light at the end of the tunnel," he said.

"Looks that way."

"Kennedy, you've been a great help."

"Really, I'm just doing my job."

"I must say I'm going to miss your company. Where have you been keeping yourself this week?" Finally. He was giving me his undivided attention.

"What do you mean?" I asked as he walked up behind me and glanced out his window, overlooking the city. Without turning around in my chair, I sensed him checking me out.

"I usually see you in the elevator or catch a glimpse of you in the lobby, but this week I didn't run into you. I looked for you. I hoped to see you.

Seeing you, even for a few seconds, always makes my day. You're a breath of fresh air."

I blushed. "Oh, I've had a lot of work to catch up on, not to mention my growing to-do list."

"Well, I hope I haven't put you behind schedule."

"No, we are unusually busy this time of the year; this is not the norm."

"This makes me appreciate you helping me out all the more." There was that perfect smile again. I shivered when I thought of those lips nibbling on my neck.

"You're welcome."

By now he had moved and was sitting in the chair across from his desk. The one usually reserved for visitors. For a moment the only sound in the room was our breathing. Self-conscious, I looked down. Drake continued to stare intensely at me.

"I really like you, Kennedy Logan. You know that? I could get into you."

I didn't comment; I didn't know what to say.

"I know this could be complicated for both of us, but I'd love to see you outside the office. I don't typically mix business and pleasure, but there's something about you that's different, worth breaking the rules for."

I didn't move.

"I can't get you off my mind. I'm seriously feeling you."

"Me either . . . I don't mix business with pleasure."

"Well, we are adults and we can handle this. There are exceptions to everything. Right? Rules are made to be broken."

I didn't respond. My thoughts were racing, bumping, colliding into each other at rapid speed.

"And I'm sure we could be discreet. No one has to know."

I glanced down at my Fossil watch. "We'd better get started. Don't you think?"

Drake glared at me for a few seconds and then he smiled that fabulous, one hundred–watt smile. The one that made my heartbeat speed up, my pulse race, and my legs quiver.

"Don't say another word. I understand. Let's get started . . . on this paperwork."

Drake and I worked diligently for the next forty-five minutes or so. I didn't want to see another stack of reports for a long, long time. We had accomplished quite a bit in a short span. Now he was joking around and telling me about some of his encounters since coming to work for our company. He had the diction and movements of some of the senior managers down to a science. He had me in stitches with his imitations. I'd never laughed so hard. I told him he missed his calling; he should have been a stand-up comedian. Our mood had quickly switched from business to playful in a matter of minutes. He took me totally off guard when he asked, "Why haven't you mentioned what happened between us?"

I hesitated and crossed my legs. "I don't know, I thought maybe I had imagined the entire thing."

"No, it definitely was real," he stated, looking at me from his spot on the edge of the desk.

"Oh," was all I could say.

"You are too funny, Kennedy. You've never done anything like that before, have you?" he asked, amused.

"No, I can't say that I have, not in a professional setting anyway."

"See, that's what's so refreshing about you. There is so much you haven't experienced. You've lived a sheltered life, Kennedy Logan."

"Well, I don't know if that's good or bad."

"It's not bad. You just need to loosen up and let go sometimes. Don't freak out over everything. Life is too short not to try to experience everything it has to offer."

"That's funny, you sound just like my friend, Taylor."

"Well, she's right. We're right," Drake proclaimed proudly.

"I'm not sure I know how to let loose. I'm pretty conservative."

"Don't worry. Stick with me. I can show you things, Miss Logan, that you wouldn't believe or couldn't perceive before."

"I bet you can, Mr. Collins," I stated, boldly flirting with him now.

"How old are you?"

"I'm twenty-eight."

"What month is your birthday?"

"June."

"Oh, so that makes you a Gemini. Y'all love hard and give your all in relationships. See, I'm up to speed on astrology."

"You are crazy," I laughed, forgetting where we were.

"Am I? I think I'm a thirty-year-old man who speaks his mind and goes after what he wants. And I want you," he stated only inches from my face now. I smelled the mint he had only a few minutes earlier popped into his mouth. "I typically get what I want."

"Really?"

"You heard me."

With that, Drake kneeled down in front of my chair. I noticed the muscles of his thighs expand and bulge against the fabric of his pants. Seconds later, while he cupped my chin and looked deep into my eyes, he moved his other hand from my ankle up to my thigh, taking my skirt with him in one swift swoosh. I instantly closed my eyes and let out a surrendering sigh. I couldn't fight this. When I opened them again, Drake had my skirt pulled up, showing off my silky red panties as his large hand rubbed and massaged between my open thigh. Already I experienced a warmness spreading and radiating within.

"Pull those off," Drake demanded.

"Pardon me?"

He laughed and repeated himself. "You heard me. Pull those off." He was whispering now. "Take off your panties."

"Somebody might walk in." I could barely think with him opening my legs and touching me.

"They won't. You do trust me, don't you?" His middle finger found my spot, as it slid underneath my panties. Dove in deep. Pulled out and pushed in with two fingers.

I nodded. With my eyes never leaving his face, I took a deep breath, stood up, and slipped my panties off and dropped them to the floor, then just stood there, not knowing what to do next.

With his hands on my shoulders, Drake slowly pushed me back down into the chair. He spread my legs as wide as they'd go and then he went to work. I allowed him to do whatever with me. I didn't fight him. I didn't protest. I didn't say no. I . . . simply . . . surrendered.

First, he placed his gorgeous face down there and gently rubbed it around. Then his tongue proceeded to do things to me that my mind had only imagined. At one point he had to put his free hand over my mouth to muffle my intense moans. Drake was relentless with his mouth and fingers. He knew exactly what to do to get my body to respond. I was putty in his hands. Mere molding clay. I couldn't move. I couldn't think. I couldn't breathe. I couldn't do anything but come.

For thirty minutes, yes, thirty minutes, Drake took me to heaven with his oral pleasure. When he added his fingers to the equation, I thought I'd go out of my freaking mind. Added to the surrealness and excitement was the fact that there was an entire floor of associates and managers, just on the other side of that door, and they had no idea what was going on.

Later, Drake had me wide open, sprawled across his desk. I was on my back with my private parts and breasts exposed and in full view for the world to see. Suddenly, there was a knock at the door.

I thought I'd die of fright and embarrassment. I froze.

Drake was cool. He actually kept pushing his fingers in and out of my womanhood. Ever so slowly. In and out. Deeper. Slowly.

"Yes?" He pushed in.

"Mr. Collins, I wanted to remind you that I'm leaving early today." It was Drake's secretary.

"See you Monday. Have a great weekend, Brenda." He pulled out. His fingers were glistening with my wetness.

"You too."

"I will," he said, inserting another finger, now four. He had me moving up and down to his finger motion as he took me to yet another orgasm while he coaxed me through.

"Yeah. That's it. Let yourself go. That's my girl," he whispered. "Tell me you love the way I make your pussy feel."

I lay back against the desktop, half on, half off, totally exhausted. Waiting for my breathing to return to normal. My chest rapidly heaving up and down.

"Tell me," he whispered near my ear. "It feels good, doesn't it?" His warm breath tickled my ear. I shivered in anticipation over his skillful fingers.

"I love the way you make me feel," I said in a monotone voice.

Drake laughed and said, "I know you do. You are so wet right now. Dripping. You enjoy me eating your pussy? Don't you?"

I remained silent. His fingers were still inside me, moving, teasing me.

"Let me hear you say pussy."

"Nooo," I squealed in horror.

"Come on," he said, moving his fingers around a bit, exploring. Opening me up.

As another spasm shook my body, I closed my eyes and shook my head.

"Just say, 'I want you to eat my pussy again, Drake,' and I'll leave you alone."

He leaned in closer. Whispered in my ear, "Say, 'Shove your tongue up my wet pussy and make me come.'"

I couldn't say it. He laughed and pulled out his fingers. He held up his index finger, showing it to me, which was drenched with my wetness.

"I bet you've never tasted yourself, either, have you?"

He didn't wait for an answer. "Come here," he stated, guiding his finger into my mouth before I could protest

"Lick it off." His eyes held mine. Waiting for me to comply.

I didn't move.

Drake pushed his fingers back inside me and pulled out.

"Lick it off, Kennedy."

He gently opened my mouth with his fingers, and I did what he told me. I proceeded to taste myself.

"That's right. Get it all," he demanded, using his free hand to play with my pussy some more, gently squeezing my clit.

"I'm going to enjoy turning you out," he whispered as he caressed my face.

"What?"

"Nothing, baby. Nothing."

With a big smile on my face, I left his office fifteen minutes later. Drake had my home and cell numbers, home address, and confirmation for a date on Saturday evening.

Chapter 12

"Hello, Kennedy Logan speaking."

"Yeah. Yeah. Yeah. Save it, save it. Girl, what's going on? You got a minute? I'm seriously stressing on my end. What are you doing?"

It was Taylor. As usual, she was going a mile a minute, showed no signs of stalling, and I couldn't get a word in edgewise.

"Working," I replied sarcastically.

"I'm so glad you're back at work because your mother wouldn't let me within one hundred feet of you. I think she set up guard duty next to your phone. I get the impression she thinks I'm a bad influence on you or something."

"Taylor, be for real. You know Mother loves you like a second daughter. She is always asking about you and how you're doing."

"Well, I wouldn't have known it the way she has treated me the last couple of weeks. Every time I called, you were always busy or resting, according to her. I didn't feel the love. Not at all. I couldn't get through on your cell; it kept going straight into voice mail."

"I lost my cell phone and haven't replaced it yet."

"You need to purchase another one. And soon."

"Taylor, you know how Mother is, and I didn't know she was screening my calls. I thought I hadn't heard from you because you were out of town on business."

"Well, now you know. Plus, when has being out of town ever stopped me from calling you?"

"True. Well, I apologize."

"Plus, I'm mad at you. I had to go to the club by myself that night you promised you would hang out."

"Oh, I'm sorry. I've had so much on my mind that I completely forgot all about that," I lied.

"I know you forgot. Of course, when I called to remind you, your mother wouldn't put me through. Said you were resting and still not feeling well."

"Did she?"

"Yes, K."

"Ump."

"Kennedy, what's going on? For real. Be straight with me."

"What do you mean?"

"I mean just what I asked, what's really going on? Why did you stay out from work this long? And why has Mrs. Logan moved in with you and is acting like your personal bodyguard? What or who does she have to protect you from?"

"Taylor, I've already told you what happened. Mother was nursing me back from the flu. Even now, my body hasn't fully recovered. I'm always tired and I've lost weight." I wondered silently, how did you inform your best friend that you almost overdosed on prescription pills because of a man?

"Kennedy, come on now. This is me you're talking to and I know how you act when you try to lie."

Silence.

"You are not very good at it."

To calm down, I breathed deeply from my nose. "Taylor, I don't feel like talking about this right now. Okay?" I felt a headache coming on.

"Knowing what a private person you are, I'm going to respect your request, but soon you gotta let me know what's going on."

"Yeah, soon."

"I'm going to hold you to that," Taylor said with determination in her voice.

"Yeah, whatever."

"Whatever, my ass. I am. I'm always in your corner and don't you forget that. That's why I'm your best friend."

"I know."

"Anyway, I'm supposed to be on a self-imposed twenty-minute break. My coworkers have gotten on my last damn nerve; everybody is tripping, so I had to take a breather. I'm gonna have to go, but I have to know one thing," Taylor said in a whisper.

"What?"

"Have you seen him yet?"

"Seen who?"

"K, what is wrong with you today? Who do you think? Drake."

"You know we broke up. I wish you'd stop worrying about me and Drake with your nosey self. No, I haven't seen him and I'm not looking for him, either."

"I'm not nosey."

"Yes, you are. You are the nosiest person I know besides Mother."

"Well, I'm in good company," she laughed.

"Whatever."

"K, you'll have to see him eventually. For God's sake, you work for the same company and department. I still can't believe you of all people got caught up in an office romance. They never work out."

"That's right. Pour more salt on my wounds."

"I'm sorry, but you're usually so practical about everything. This romance was so uncharacteristic of you."

"I guess Drake was very persuasive."

"Just don't let him sweet-talk you, change your mind, and draw you back into his life and his bed. His dick is not gold. If it is, break me off a piece so that I can cash it in."

"I won't, Mother. Now stop bugging me."

"Kennedy, I know you and you didn't stop loving that man overnight. You don't give your love away frivolously. You're vulnerable right now and Drake realizes that. So, be wary of that slimy snake in the grass."

"I will. I promise. Now, enough."

"Drake doesn't deserve you."

"That's what you and Mother keep telling me," I cited.

"It's true. You're too good for him. You always were and always will be."

I didn't respond one way or the other.

"Hello?"

"I'm here."

"K, I have to run; we have our weekly team meeting in a few minutes. I'll talk to you later. Maybe we can do lunch one day this week and play catch-up."

"Cool. Let me know because I have something I want to ask you," I answered as we said our good-byes and hung up. My mind was reeling back to what Taylor had said: the exact same thing Drake had stated what seemed like eons ago. I would have to see him sooner or later. Hopefully, it would be later, much later. Like when hell froze over.

Until glancing down at my watch, I didn't realize how

late it was, and I hadn't eaten lunch. It was already
one thirty. That explained why my stomach was growl-
ing like an angry bear and doing double somersaults.
I opened my bottom desk drawer and pulled out my
crinkled brown paper bag that contained a ham and
cheese sandwich, a pickle, chips, and bottled water.
Not exciting, but it'd do to quench the hungries. I knew
I should have listened to Mother and taken some leftovers from last night's dinner of lasagna, French bread,
and salad.

I had been back at work for almost a week now and
was just going through the motions. It was a good thing
that I knew my job backward and forward because
my mind wasn't in it. Mother had hinted that maybe
I should go back to school for my master's degree;
she said that she'd provide for me financially, and I
wouldn't have to work. She even suggested that I could
move back in with her to save on expenses. No way.

My first day back, my manager was glad to see my
return, as she promptly handed me a laundry list of
tasks to complete. Thankfully, not too many questions
were asked regarding my absence. Everyone pretty
much accepted my story about the flu and me needing
some time off due to a family emergency. My workload
hadn't diminished in my absence, so the workweek
flew by quickly.

Most of the managers on the sixth floor were out and
about servicing regional accounts. Many of my coworkers were complaining because they weren't able to get
in touch with certain managers, due to their travel.
Drake was one of them. I said a silent prayer because I
knew I wasn't strong enough to face him just yet. Still,
since I didn't know when he'd return from out-of-town

travel, I played it careful by staying close to my floor and in the safe haven of my cubicle.

Today, I was going to take my lunch and eat in an empty office around the corner from my space. It offered privacy and got me off the open floor. I needed to relax and free my mind. It had been awhile since I had last written in my journal and I wanted to vent. It did help to see everything in black and white. It put life into perspective. I couldn't believe I was writing down these things I did, but I had to accept partial blame because Drake didn't place a gun to my head.

Dear Journal,

After Drake turned me out orally, it was on. My body had never felt that way before. And we hadn't even had actual sexual intercourse. Imagine that. Yes, I was already whipped.

When I came in Drake's office chair from just his mouth and fingers, I was like, "Damn." I jumped at the chance to see him over the weekend and find out more about this exciting, mysterious, and sexy man.

Our first date was beyond unbelievable. I felt like Cinderella at the ball with her black Prince Charming in tow. If I didn't think I was in lust with the man before, by the end of our first date I knew that I definitely was seeing stars and hearing sweet violins playing our song; I was sprung. A night out on the town turned into a two-day date. That was one thing I would learn about Drake, he never did anything halfway. He did everything in a big, dramatic way. Drake was very passionate about everything: his career, his hobbies, his woman.

I thought we were simply going out to the movies and then dinner. Therefore, I dressed in a nice but casual dress and heels. We ended up going to an early dinner out in Buckhead, catching a play at the Fox Theater, and capping the night off by going for a horse-and-carriage ride through Midtown. It was magical. It was perfect. Then to top off all that excitement and my natural high, Drake had reserved a room for us at the Georgian Terrace Hotel, directly across from the Fox Theater. I was totally speechless.

I just adored this man who was able to so easily take control of any given situation. Drake was a man who took charge, and that excited me in the beginning. I noticed the envious looks women gave me when I went out with him. I didn't care; Drake was my man. And I was his woman . . . or so I thought.

Our room came complete with a Jacuzzi, king-sized bed, colorful flowers, expensive champagne, and a great view of the city. Drake didn't forget anything; he attended to the smallest of details. That was impressive. Of course, I hadn't packed an overnight bag, but he came prepared. The man was amazing. He had secretly packed a small suitcase for both of us that he had hidden in the trunk of his car. He purchased a toothbrush, toothpaste, and other essentials. He even purchased a sexy purple teddy, his favorite color, for me to sleep in. Not that it stayed on very long.

That night, Drake and I ordered room service after deciding to have a midnight snack of assorted cheese and crackers, and we sipped on chilled champagne. Drake gave what I thought was a heartfelt toast to having me in his life. Afterward, he didn't rush to get me in bed or attempt to get intimate with me. We actually cuddled on the cozy bed and talked. With my head on his stomach, I learned quite a bit about his upbringing.

He had been given a lot on a silver platter. Don't get me wrong. He worked hard for everything he received, but his parents owned a sports apparel manufacturing plant in Los Angeles. Money wasn't an issue for him. He grew up with his mother, father, one sister, and a brother. He attended private schools, excelled academically and in sports, and dated girls from affluent families. His family even owned a summer home. After graduating from college and working for the family-owned business for a few years, he wanted to branch out on his own for a change. Be his own man. Test his wings. He had heard so much about Atlanta that it was his first choice.

Literally, as the sun was rising over the city, we made the most delicious, sweetest love. Slow and easy. I felt Drake down to my soul. He made me understand and appreciate the meaning of feeling like a woman. With every touch, I grew to crave him. He made love to my entire body, mind, and soul. Drake didn't rush; he reveled in loving and caressing every inch of me. He asked what felt good. He watched to gauge my reaction to things he did to me. Drake wanted to possess me. I wanted him to love me. And love and possession don't mix. . . .

By Saturday morning we were so tired that we

slept, wrapped in each other's arms, until almost noon. I never imagined being so safe and protected. After I woke up to tender kisses, we made love two more times, took our showers, and had a light lunch in one of the restaurants downstairs. The salmon salad with iced tea was excellent. After checkout, we weren't ready to part company, so we rode out to Lenox Mall and shopped for a couple of hours. We giggled, held hands, and French kissed like two teenagers. Drake bought me a gorgeous Coach bag. It didn't matter that the price tag was almost $2,000; he didn't bat an eye at the price. When he declared that he had to have his woman dressed to the nines, I beamed because I knew he was claiming me as his woman. He had already claimed and tamed my pussy.

Yeah, that was the best date ever. It was perfect. Unfortunately, Drake wasn't. Not by a long shot. However, it took months for me to discover that tidbit of information. That revelation would have saved me so much heartache and pain. Looking back, the signs were there. Hindsight is twenty-twenty.

Chapter 13

"Hey, I'm in the lobby. Come on down, girl. I'm starving," Taylor screamed into the phone, hanging up before I could manage more than a simple greeting.

"I'll be right down," I said to a dead line.

Today was Valentine's Day, and I almost didn't come to work. I seriously contemplated calling in sick. I didn't feel like seeing my coworkers' cubicles overflowing with beautiful red roses and cards, or hearing them boast about what their boyfriends or husbands were doing for them, or where they were taking them for Valentine's Day.

It seemed everyone was in a relationship or had that special someone in their life to love them, but me. I had no one. I was all alone. Drake was history after what happened that night.

Even Taylor, who went through men like ruined and discarded stockings, had been dating this one guy on a regular basis. Regular for Taylor meant for more than a month. I have to admit, I was more than a bit jealous. Sometimes, I wished I were more like her. Taylor was outgoing, chipper, and gorgeous. I don't think she ever met anyone who wasn't a friend. She was the type of person who would strike up a conversation in an elevator with a complete stranger, while most of us would be staring at the ceiling or the doors and waiting for them to open. Taylor would walk off the elevator with a business card and plans to hook up later at happy hour.

After making it down to the lobby, stepping off the elevator, and glancing toward the gold and black security desk, I spotted Taylor right away. She was hard to miss. With a dress that was fierce, but not too sexy for work, she was dressed from head to toe in red. She had on red shoes (which I'm sure cost her a small fortune) with straps that enclosed her ankles.

Her long brown hair was pulled back off her face and cascaded in waves down her back. Taylor would tell you in a minute that her hair wasn't a weave, either. Don't even think it. Resembling a young Janet Jackson, she looked gorgeous. However, Taylor always looked great, like she just stepped off the pages of a fashion magazine or perhaps a catwalk in Paris.

The thin and very married security guard closest to her was trying to check her out without being too obvious. Taylor was too busy checking her lipstick and hair in her small compact to notice him. Yet, all the men passing by noticed her and gave admiring stares, and no doubt wished they'd be lucky enough to spend even one night with her.

After putting her compact away, she looked up and spotted me. Instantly, a huge smile spread across her face. A smile that lit up her deep dimples. Her happiness made me grin, and I momentarily forgot my situation. Taylor met me halfway and linked her left arm through my right one.

"Hey, sweetie," she said, giving me a quick kiss on the cheek. "Happy Valentine's Day."

"Is it? I wouldn't know," I stated glumly.

"Oh, Kennedy, come on. It's not that bad. Today is just another day. A day for big corporations to make money off of the buying public who get caught up in yet another holiday. Next month it will be Easter."

"That's easy for you to say. I bet your new boyfriend, what's his name, hooked you up."

Taylor didn't say anything, just continued confidently walking toward the revolving doors to the outside.

"Well?" I asked, stopping halfway out the door.

"Okay, Kennedy, I did receive some flowers. But so what?"

"Someone in the world cares about you. That's what."

"I care about you and so do your parents."

"Thanks, but it's just not the same," I declared, walking outside.

"Well, I'm going to put a smile on that pretty face of yours if it kills me. What do you want to eat?"

"I don't care. Food is food. I'll go wherever you want to go."

"See what I mean? K, you have to start making decisions. Quit being so indecisive. That's why Drake bossed you around."

"Whatever."

"I'm treating you to lunch, I haven't seen you in weeks, and here you are, acting funky. Snap out of it."

"Well, thanks a lot. We can't all be the charming, sexy lady in red," I stated sarcastically.

"What am I going to do with you?" Taylor said, pretending to be disgusted.

I rolled my eyes upward. Before I could answer, Taylor was off on another tirade.

"Since you can't decide, I'll choose for us. Let's walk over to Mick's for lunch. I've been feening for some of their chocolate chip cheesecake. I haven't had any in months."

"It doesn't matter. Sounds good to me."

"Okay, cool. Let's do it. Ooh, I'm so happy to see you," she declared, squeezing me into a gentle hug, I admit I was thrilled to see her as well.

As we walked the couple of blocks up to Mick's, Taylor was a complete chatterbox. I couldn't help but notice the appreciative glances and outright stares that were directed our way. Whenever Taylor and I hung out, men seemed to come out of the woodwork like roaches.

As for Taylor, I couldn't recall when she didn't have a man she was dating, or one or two waiting in the wings. I met plenty of men, but I guess my personality spoke volumes for me. Men saw me as standoffish and I wasn't into dating every Jamal, Brandon, and Malik who asked me out. I was looking for quality, not quantity. Taylor, on the other hand, was following her mother's example. By the time I met her, Taylor's mother had already gone through four husbands. That simple fact made for some deep, late-night, heartfelt conversations during our college years.

"Here we are. Crowded as usual, just as we expected," Taylor said, opening the door for us to enter. As always, the noise level was in maximum overdrive. We had to nearly scream to hear what the other was saying.

"Table for two," she requested to the friendly waiter dressed in black and white.

Taylor and I were in luck because we were immediately led to a booth near the kitchen, over in the corner of the busy restaurant. I didn't have to study the menu since I had eaten at Mick's on numerous occasions, but I pretended to check out the selections to shield myself from her scrutiny and pending questions. As I pretended to peruse the menu, I could feel her eyes on me.

"Well, friend, what's up? Looks like you've lost some weight," Taylor said, carefully looking me over.

I didn't respond one way or the other. I knew it was only a matter of time before the fifty questions began.

"And don't tell me nothing's up because I know better."

"I'm sorry to disappoint you, but nothing is up."

"Kennedy, I've been your best friend for how many years? I can sense when something is bothering you," she said, squeezing my hand across the table. "I love you. When you hurt, I hurt."

After hearing the sincerity in Taylor's voice, I had to close my eyes tight because I longed to tell her everything that was wrong in my world. I wanted to inform her of my unhappiness with myself and my failed relationship with Drake. I longed for her to know of my attempted suicide and how Mother was smothering me with her unwavering love and devotion.

I ached to ask why I couldn't find love, only sorrow, and to ask why my life wasn't going the way I wanted it to go. I yearned to tell her how I daydreamed about finding my birth mother and asking her why she gave me up. There was so much I desperately needed to share with Taylor as she sat there with her perfect manicure, expertly lined M•A•C lips, beautifully coiffed hair. But I didn't; I simply couldn't.

I lied and told her half-truths because the real truth hurt too deeply. My truths weren't pretty, and I wanted to be pretty in her eyes. I didn't want to disappoint Taylor or take the smile from her lips. Her smile let me know that there was joy in life. It wasn't impossible.

"Taylor, so much is going on. It would take three lunches to discuss everything and fill you in."

"I have time. I have all the time in the world for you, K."

"I know and I appreciate it."

"Girl, is Drake still bothering you?"

At first I didn't speak. I just looked ahead of me and stared at the wall.

"Well, is he?" Taylor asked impatiently.

I had to let some of my confusion out. "Not lately. But I can't get him off my mind. I have a love-hate relationship playing out in my head and heart. I despise how he treated me, which is what caused our relationship to end; yet I still love him when I think of all the good times we shared. And, yes, Taylor, we did share many wonderful times," I declared, staring at her and praying that she'd understand where I was coming from.

"I know, sweetie. I'm sure you did. I know you are hurting now, but there are more fish in the sea if you'd only give them a chance. Drake wasn't the one. He wasn't right for you. He was more like a piranha. I don't know what happened to permanently end your relationship, but I assume you will tell me in time. I'm just glad he's out of your life. For good."

"Yeah, you're right."

"What can I do? What can I do to help?"

"Nothing. I just need time to see where I wanna be."

"Take it. Take that time."

I didn't say anything, just looked up as our waiter approached the table with pen and pad in hand.

"Are you lovely ladies ready to order?"

Taylor answered for us. "Yes. I think we are."

We placed our orders and settled into a comfortable silence, as friends do.

"Kennedy, you know I don't usually get involved in your love life."

"Since when?" I asked in astonishment.

"I want to discuss Drake. I don't like how he treated you."

"Here we go again."

"Yes, here we go again. When you love someone, you just don't treat them bad."

"He is no longer in my life. Between you and Mother, y'all are driving me crazy over Drake Collins."

"Well, maybe you should listen to us. Underneath all that bullshit charm and good looks, he is an arrogant, conniving, good-for-nothing, lowlife. I think he secretly hates women," Taylor exclaimed in her usual animated way with hands and hair flying all over the place.

"You really don't like him, do you?" I asked with a genuine smile on my face.

"No, I don't and I don't feel that you . . ." Taylor stopped mid-sentence when she realized I was making fun of her.

We laughed for a good two minutes.

For the remainder of lunch, my mood soared. It was good to be back in Taylor's presence. Her aura was so positive and full of intoxicating energy. She was perfect for her role as an account executive over at Coca-Cola. I needed to bask in her presence so that some of her upbeat energy would rub off on me.

"Are we still going away in June?" Taylor asked out of the blue.

"I don't know. I hadn't thought about it. Maybe."

"What do you mean maybe? You can't break with tradition."

"Well, yeah, I guess you're right. I'm going."

"Oh, oh. And we have to go shopping for swimwear."

"I'll wear my suit from last year."

"No. We have to pick out something new and sexy. Something that will make the men fall out their lounge chairs with their tongues dragging on the ground."

"Maybe I don't want them falling out of their chairs over me."

"K, you are no fun. That's the thrill—to see how stupid and juvenile they act just to see a little ass and cleavage."

"That's your idea of fun?"

"Yes. I'm seriously thinking about writing a book called *1001 Stupid Men Tricks*. I've seen enough dumb shit at the clubs to fill up two books."

"I wouldn't have enough material for a quarter of a book."

"K, you've got to get out more and be more observant. You've never noticed how you can simply bat your long eyelashes, toss your hair a couple of times, look at men with those big innocent eyes you have, and they are at your beck and call."

"No, I haven't noticed."

"See what I mean? Jamaica, here we come. Girl, I heard that those island men have the biggest dicks. Something about the weather there."

"Girl, you are so stupid," I said, exploding into laughter again.

"What? What did I say?" Taylor asked with confusion on her face.

"Something about the weather. What kind of theory is that?"

"Yeah, the weather and their diet grow them longer and thicker than U.S. men. K, I'm serious. I saw that on a documentary or somewhere."

"Yeah, right. Do you realize how ridiculous you sound?"

"Seriously, it was Public Broadcast TV. They wouldn't lie."

Taylor and I looked at each other and went into another round of uncontrollable giggles. Taylor was laughing so hard that she had to reach for her water and take a sip when she started choking.

For as long as I could remember, Taylor and I always went away the second week in June. It was a tradition we started right after college. We would do the girl thing, pack our swimsuits and sunscreen and head off for a wonderful week full of fun and sun. We would always re-bond during those times and I would realize all over again what a true and real friend Taylor was. I knew she could say the same about me. We had some really deep conversations during those times and, of course, we'd party.

Our waiter brought our meals and drinks to the table and went to greet new customers seated at his other stations.

"Sweetie, how's your salad?" Taylor asked, digging into her lunch with gusto. "It's good."

"Well, you're not eating like it's good. You are barely touching your food. We've got to get those pounds back on you."

"Yes, Mother."

"Men don't like twigs. A sistah got to have some meat for a brotha to hold on to."

"Yes, Mother. I hear you, Mother."

Taylor gave me this look like she wanted to say something but then stopped. Just like she knew me well, I knew her too.

"What? Spit it out. I know that look anywhere. Say what's on your mind. You always do."

"Okay, as much as I love your mother, when is she going home? I know she means well, but don't you miss your independence?"

"Soon, she's leaving soon." I hoped that was the case. Mother still didn't trust me living alone. She didn't verbally express this, but I knew.

"Hell, your flu symptoms are gone. Tell Mommy Dearest she has gots to go. Hit the road."

We looked at each other and within seconds fell out laughing again. Mommy Dearest was Taylor's pet name for my mother. Of course, she didn't say it to her face, but Taylor coined it back in college. Even though it came from the movie with the same name, I didn't get offended by it. We both knew that Mother's intentions were well meant even if they were annoying at times.

After taking a long lunch, I was actually feeling better. Better than I had felt in a while. Taylor is good for me. She had me cracking up with her antics and good nature. At one point she was feeding me pieces of my grilled chicken Caesar salad with her fork.

"Come on, open up. Here comes the choo choo. Oh, I forgot to ask you, how's your Coke?"

"Delicious, ice cold, and packed full of caffeine and sugar."

"Good. Well, let's make a toast to Drake. And then you must order another one."

We held our glasses up and clicked. Taylor had witnessed Drake's tirades over me drinking Cokes. I'd come to realize it wasn't an issue of my health; it was an issue of control with Drake.

"Good riddance."

"Ditto."

We were laughing our heads off, being silly and giddy. It felt so good to laugh. In passing, our waiter asked if we had slipped some liquor into our cherry sodas. We giggled even more. But like they say, all good things must come to an end. I glanced down at my watch and realized I had overstayed my lunch hour and my voice mail probably held dozens of missed calls.

Suddenly, I noticed the atmosphere at our table had changed; it became ice cold. I glanced up at Taylor and saw her staring toward the entrance.

"What's wrong?"

Since my back was to the door, I turned in my seat to see what had stolen her attention and evidently her good mood along with it.

I froze and my hands literally started shaking as Drake's eyes met mine. I could see the familiar specks of green dancing in his pupils. Taylor sensed my immediate distress.

"Calm down, Kennedy. Be cool. We can leave," she whispered between clenched teeth. "Just stay cool."

"Yeah, let's go. Now," I barely muttered.

"Shit. His ass showing up made me miss getting my slice of cheesecake," Taylor nearly screamed in anger.

As Taylor attempted to pay the check and leave a tip, Drake approached our table with a huge smirk on his face. He was looking as handsome as ever in his gray pinstriped suit, and it looked like he had gotten some sun because his skin tone was radiant. He didn't look like a man who was pining over his woman or the loss of a doomed relationship.

"Hello, ladies. You two are a sight for sore eyes. Two beautiful ladies at one table. Today must be my lucky day."

Taylor answered, "I wish I could say the same because my eyes have seen enough."

"Taylor, how are you? Good to see you too," he said sarcastically. "I see your attitude hasn't changed. Still sucks."

"No. I'm still not willing to let you treat me like a second-class citizen. I don't think you could handle a woman who has a mind of her own."

"I believe you think you are a man, with balls and all."

"And if I do, then I'm still a better one than you could ever hope to be."

Drake ignored her and directed his full attention to me.

"Happy Valentine's Day, Kennedy. I started to send you some flowers, but then I remembered how you kicked me to the curb. You and I must talk," he stated, reaching over to touch my left shoulder.

"Don't. Don't touch me. Don't you ever place your hands on me again," I managed to utter through clenched teeth as I pulled away like his touch was fire.

"You heard her," Taylor screamed, pushing Drake out of the way and making her way from our table. "Keep the fuck away from her, you arrogant son of a bitch."

Following her, I sideswiped people in my path and was almost out the front door when I barely heard Drake call out, "Kennedy, we will talk. That's a promise. You can't run from me forever." When I glanced back, our waiter and Drake were staring at us. There was amusement on Drake's face and disbelief on our waiter's.

On our brisk walk back to my building, Taylor managed to calm me down a little.

"K, don't give that man your power. I don't know what went down with you guys, but Drake is obviously getting joy out of your pain. Don't let him. Don't give him the satisfaction."

"All I did was love that man. That's all."

"I know, sweetie, but sometimes love isn't enough. He'll miss you one day. He'll realize what he lost in you, and you'll understand what you have to offer a *real* man. In time your heart will heal."

We had made it back to the front of my building, and all I wanted to do was walk the two blocks to my car and drive home.

"Let's sit here for a minute," she stated, gesturing toward an empty bench.

I reluctantly slumped down beside her.

"I'm serious, K. Don't let Drake deflate your spirit. I don't know what happened, but don't let him break you. Okay?"

"Okay."

"Good. That's the Kennedy I know and love." Taylor smiled. "You had mentioned you wanted to talk with me about something. Now is as good a time as any." She looked at her watch. "I still have some time before I definitely have to be back."

Sitting there beside Taylor, I sensed the love radiating all around her and I knew I could confide in her because I realized our friendship was genuine. It was the real deal.

I hesitated only a moment. "You know that I'm adopted, that has never been a secret, but I don't think I've ever mentioned my desire to find my birth mom."

"No, you haven't, but I can see how you would have a natural desire to know your roots and I'm sure you have tons of questions for your birth mom. I know I would."

In that moment, I realized I had been right in revealing my plans. She would support me.

"I'm torn because I don't want Mother to think I don't love her, because I do, with all my heart, but I have so many questions that have gone unanswered. Then again, I don't want to betray Mother or Daddy."

"Kennedy, your mother only wants what is best for you. That's the bottom line. She loves you and I don't think she would take it as an act of betrayal on your part."

"I guess you're right."

She nodded and smiled again. "I am right."

"I wanted to ask you if you'd help me with the process of locating her, my birth mother."

"Girl, of course. I feel honored, but that was a given. Did you really have to ask me that?"

I audibly sighed a sound of relief.

"Are you feeling better now?" Taylor asked, looking me over.

"A little."

"Well, that's a start."

I glanced at my watch this time. "I'd better get back."

"Listen, K," Taylor said. "Call me if you need me. I have a two o'clock meeting, but I should be at my desk after three o'clock, no later than three fifteen."

"I will."

"I mean it. Call me."

"Thanks for lunch."

"K, you are gonna be all right. Time heals all wounds. That and a new man with a big dick."

She laughed. I didn't.

As I headed into the building, I didn't look back. I tried to walk tall and confident. If I turned around, Taylor would see the beginnings of new tears forming in my eyes. I didn't want her to see how weak I was. I used the ride up in the elevator to mentally compose myself. I somehow made it through work for the rest of the day and managed to make it safe and sound through rush-hour traffic. All I could think about was my bed; it was my single focus. As soon as I entered my apartment, I was thankful that Mother wasn't around as I left a track of clothes down the hallway. I stayed up long enough to write an entry in my journal before I was in bed with the covers pulled tightly over my head. In big red letters, I wrote:

Dear Journal,

Today was not a very good day. In fact, today was one of the worst in a while. When I saw Drake at Mick's, I wanted to die again. With him standing there, gloating down at me, I felt smaller than miniscule. I hate that man. I despise him so much. What does he want to talk about? There's nothing more to say. We are history, ka-put, done. After what he did, there's nothing more to discuss. I hate him for that. Absolutely hate his ass.

Happy Valentine's Day. Yeah, right.

Chapter 14

Sunday afternoon found me still in my pj's. I didn't feel like showering, dressing, eating, or doing anything. I simply didn't have the energy or the desire. I didn't understand why I let him get to me. There is always that one person who can just get under your skin. Drake was mine.

Even Mother couldn't persuade me to attend church service with her at New Hope Baptist Church. As much as I loved to hear their choir sing, I just couldn't get up. I finally crept out of bed because I had slept more this weekend than any one person was humanly capable of.

I hated myself for acting like the lead female character in one of the many African American relationship books I read. It's cool to read about somebody else going through drama, but it's another story when it pertains to you. Lately, my life consisted of relationship woes, drama, sex, and more drama.

Strolling into the living room, I absently turned on the TV and flipped through some magazines that were lying on the coffee table. I had gotten so behind in my reading of *Ebony, Essence, Today's Black Woman,* and *O Magazine* that they were piled up. Briefly, I thought about fixing myself something to eat, more out of habit than anything else, but I couldn't muster the energy to get off the sofa.

I did have one bit of good news. Mother informed me that she was thinking about moving back home. She felt that things were going well with me and she could check in on me over the weekends. I was happy because I craved my independence and personal space back.

I didn't catch her secretly staring at me as much as she did after my situation. Around Mother, I tried to put on a happy face, so I guess she probably thought I was okay. And I was. I still had my bouts with depression, but I had no intentions of harming myself in any shape, form, or fashion in the near future. It was absolutely crazy what I had attempted to do. Never again.

With remote in hand, I crashed on my sofa and pulled a flannel blanket over my body. When the phone rang, I was channel surfing and replaying over and over in my mind my reaction to Drake in the restaurant. At first I wasn't going to answer it, I didn't want to be bothered, but at the last minute I picked it up.

"Hello?"

"Hello there, baby girl."

"Daddy?"

"Yes, your one and only," he proudly proclaimed. I heard the smile in his Southern drawl and it touched my heart. I missed him so much. There was a time Daddy could do no wrong in my eyes. I'd wanted to find and marry a man just like him. That was before he walked out and left Mother for a younger woman. Though I never admitted it to him, daddy disappointed me. You don't give up on a lifetime of marriage without a fight.

"What a surprise. We don't usually talk this much in one month," I said, curling my legs underneath me as I sat up on the sofa, and made myself more comfortable as I pulled the blanket around me.

"Well, you were on my mind. In fact, you've been on my mind a lot lately."

"Really?"

"Yes. Is everything all right with you, baby girl?" he asked with concern clearly etched in his voice.

"Yes, Daddy. Why would you ask that?" I asked, starting to feel a little nervous. I knew he couldn't possibly be aware of what had occurred.

"I don't know. I can't explain it, but . . . I'm just glad you're doing well. I want you to be happy."

"I am. How's life treating you?" I asked, quickly changing the subject.

"It could be better."

"What do you mean by that? Is something wrong, Daddy?" I could clearly hear sadness in his tone that I hadn't noticed before.

"Don't tell that mother of yours because I'm sure she'll gloat for the next forty years, but Loretta left me."

"What? You're kidding, right?"

"No, baby girl, I wish I were. She woke up one morning and out of the blue told me that we weren't working out anymore. Said I was sapping away what was left of her youth. Said I made her feel old beyond her years and she was tired of people mistaking me for her daddy."

"Wow. Loretta said that? I'm so sorry, Daddy."

"No. Don't be, baby girl. Months ago I knew our relationship had started on a downhill spiral when she starting spending an enormous amount of time away from home, at the local gym. Loretta is not the type who is into fitness that way. She told me she needed her space."

"Oh."

"It got to the point where we were more like roommates than lovers. I saw her in passing."

"Really?"

"This is a pretty small town and I started hearing rumors."

"That's unbelievable."

"Well, Loretta had herself a male personal trainer at the gym and I discovered he got a little more personal than necessary."

"I'm sorry, Daddy."

"Don't be. Life goes on. No matter how hurt you may be, life doesn't stop for your pain. You live and you learn and you're never too old to learn a new lesson. Remember that."

"I will."

"You suck up the pain and get through it. Don't ever give up on the beauty and joys life has to offer; they far outweigh the disappointments. God can get us through anything life may toss our way."

I listened.

"Don't get me wrong. Loretta has been gone for over a week now and it hurt when she moved out, still does. Our apartment feels so empty. We built a decent life for ourselves during the last five years. However, it just wasn't enough for her; I wasn't enough."

"I don't know what to say."

"Sweetie, you don't have to say anything; sometimes being an ear to listen is golden. In some ways, I was relieved she left because Loretta was never your mother. Couldn't clean or cook worth a damn. She never ironed or folded my clothes the right way or bought and cooked my favorite foods. It's funny because when she left, it made me think about how your mother must have felt when I walked out."

"I don't . . ."

"It's true. What goes around comes around."

"That's what they say. Karma has a way of evening out the score."

"Baby girl, I can only imagine what your mother has said about me since I left. Some of it is probably true and well deserved. Just know I never wanted to bring you into our situation, or hurt anyone, you or your mother. But I know this has been hard on you, whether you care to admit it or not."

"Daddy, don't—"

"And, I'm sorry, baby. I truly am," he cried. "I know you are all grown up, but you are still my baby and always will be."

"Daddy, there's no need for you to apologize to me. It's your life and you have to live it the way you see fit. You can't worry about what other people think." I realized I was repeating his words to him. "You only get one chance."

"You're right. Even if I came out looking like a fool in the end, which I did, this was something I had to do. Your mother was all I had ever known. I loved her, but I felt cheated and trapped. I owed it to myself to see what else was out there," he ranted on like he had to rationalize his actions to himself. "The grass always seems greener on the other side."

"Um-huh."

"Speaking of the number one nagger herself, what has she been up to lately? Believe it or not, I actually picked up the phone the other night and almost dialed her number." He chuckled lightly at just the thought.

"Really?" I was thinking that he wouldn't have found her there, and if he had, he wouldn't have cared to hear what Mother had to say. She would have given him an earful and then some. It would not have been cute.

"Yeah, but at the last minute, I came to my senses," he laughed. "How's old gal doing?"

"Mother's doing fine."

"She spending time with anybody?"

"You have to ask her."

"Oh, I guess you have strict orders not to discuss her with your old man?"

"Something like that."

"I should have known." He chuckled again and coughed. "She still baking those peach cobblers and serving up her golden fried chicken by the buckets?"

"You know it, that will never change. Daddy, hang in there. Okay?"

"Just talking with you has made me feel one hundred percent better. And it's been too long. I'm gonna have to come up there and see my baby girl face-to-face. Give you a big ol' hug and kiss."

"I would like that because you're right, it has been too long."

"Listen, tell your mother I said hello and hopefully one day soon she'll find it in her heart to forgive me. Okay, sugar?"

"I will, Daddy. I love you."

"I love you back. I'll talk to you soon."

"Bye."

"Take care."

After chatting with Daddy, I hung up the phone with a new, solid resolve. I realized no matter how old we get, we can still make mistakes. But as long as we have the wisdom to view them for what they truly are, we can move past them, learn from them, and overcome any challenges we face.

I decided then and there, on the spot, that I was going to stop the pity party, confront and acknowledge my mistakes, and look toward a happy future. I deserved happiness. My first stop was confronting Drake. It was time to stop being a coward.

Dear Journal,

Sometimes I close my eyes and dream of the day when Drake will love me. However, it's just that, a dream . . . a carefully crafted illusion. I used to think I needed him next to me. Sometimes, I craved him so much I couldn't sleep at night. Thoughts of him kept me at full alert. Drake was my natural high.

Now, that's never going to happen—Drake loving me. There are situations and events that occur in one's life that never allow you to go back. There aren't any what-ifs, buts, or ands. Some things are totally unforgettable, unacceptable, and unforgivable. In some situations, saying "I'm sorry" is simply not enough. Not good enough. The only feasible solution is to go your own, separate ways because hate is your constant companion.

We were once happy though, at least I was. I'll admit that. Drake, I think he was happy with me. At first anyway. There were many smiles, gentle moments in time, sincere mutterings of truths. I hope everything wasn't a lie. However, I know, once you tell one lie, you have to continue to keep up with the first one. Eventually, your reality be-

comes based on a myriad of lies on top of lies, and that's no way to live. You're simply existing under an illusion of untruths.

I figured out, much too late, that Drake is all about the chase. The thrill of the game. He gets off on making women love him. That gives him an adrenaline rush. Once that's accomplished, he's gone . . . like a thief in the night. Game over. He is very competitive by nature. Love, just like business, is all about dividing, conquering, and winning. Once it's accomplished, it's another notch on his belt. Another line or two on his glorious resume. Broken hearts his souvenir.

Drake realizes he is very attractive, gorgeous even, a charming man, and most women's fantasy. He uses that to his advantage. He has cultivated it to an exact science that turns women to putty in his strong hands, and then he attempts to mold and sculpture that clay to his heart's desire.

So yes, in the beginning we were happy. Very happy. Drake wouldn't have had it any other way. It was all part of the illusion he expertly crafted. In order to love him, you have to be happy first. And believe me, Drake knows how to make a woman feel special and desired. Special, intimate dinners, weekly deliveries of fresh, fragrant flowers, luxurious weekend getaways, whispered promises during midnight phone calls, "just because" cards that speak of love and devotion; these were all part of that total facade to make one love him. He succeeded.

I thought Drake was the one who could make my life complete. Now, I think that whole concept is totally ludicrous and I was crazy for thinking it. Neither Drake nor anyone else can make my life complete. I have to do that for myself. I didn't come to this realization overnight; I won't give myself that much credit. It took a near fatal mistake, reflecting, and growing up.

Looking back, I was at Drake's beck and call. I'd drop everything to be with him. My family, friends, even myself, played second fiddle to Drake. It used to upset Taylor so much when I'd break an outing with her to be with Drake. All Drake had to say was jump and I'd ask how high. I had no shame. Drake became my entire world, and that's when he became dangerous to my soul and well-being. Never make a man your entire world. Don't give him that power.

"Kennedy, I could stay like this forever," Drake whispered, leaning down and kissing me on the forehead. His body was warm and solid. I felt protected, secure, wanted, and loved.

"Me too," I barely answered with closed eyes. I was still coming off my high. We had made love and I was relishing the moments before the sweetness fled into the darkness and cover of night. Candlelight flickered off the walls in my bedroom, creating strange shadows in their wake. And there was a strong and strange mixture of berries and sex that clung to the air.

Drake was slowly tracing his fingers up and down my arm. Each touch sent shivers throughout my being. And lying wrapped in his arms, I felt happy.

"How you feeling?" he asked.

"Great, babe, as always. You?"

"Satisfied."

"I love you, babe."

"Ditto."

"Ditto. What does that mean?"

"You're special to me. You know that, Kennedy." He was still tracing patterns on my arm. Up and down.

"Special?" I questioned with a pout.

"I've dated a lot of women in my past, but you, you are, by a long shot, different and very special."

"How many are a lot of women?" I asked jokingly, but curious at the same time. I rose up on one elbow so I could clearly see his face.

"Oh, come on, Kennedy, I've told you of my past. I've never had a problem meeting women. Women are always throwing themselves and their pussies at me. You are with me now. You're my woman. So, it doesn't matter how many," he said, slightly agitated. The candlelight cast dark, contorted shadows across his face.

"You're right, babe," I crooned, relaxing back into his arms. *"Wait a minute. Different? Is that good or bad?"* I laughed, pulling myself up to look into his eyes again. Drake had the sexiest eyes. A woman could get lost in them, and before she knew it, she could simply drown. Sometimes I felt like I was drowning in his presence. I couldn't breathe or catch my breath.

"Baby, of course different in a good way. It couldn't possibly be in a bad way."

"How am I different, babe?"

"You really want to know?" he asked, absently cupping my breast in his hand. "You really, really want to know?" he asked, ticking my side.

"Yes, seriously, I want to know." The moment was perfect. A light rain had started to fall outside, and my apartment was warm and cozy on the inside.

"Well. For one, you don't try to be the man."

"What?" I laughed. "You're joking, right?"

"There are too many women who are kidding themselves and thinking that they can do it all, have it all, all without a man."

"What's wrong with that?"

"Baby, a man wants his woman to need him. He doesn't want to feel like he's not wanted or appreciated or needed. There can only be one leader in a relationship. The man."

"I see." I was hearing this theory for the first time.

"Women in Atlanta are notorious for that type of bullshit, feminist attitude. 'I don't need a man; a man can't do anything for me that I can't do for myself.' Bullshit. Then why are they at the club with a dress on two sizes too small showing all their ass, leaving absolutely nothing to the imagination? Why are they always in search of some dick? Answer that. Well, you aren't like that."

"Are you saying I'm not independent?"

"No, baby. I'm merely saying you act like a woman. You are content with letting me be your man. Your girl Taylor could learn from you, too."

"What? How did Taylor get brought into this conversation?"

"I don't care for Taylor, and it's obvious that she doesn't care for me either. Taylor thinks her shit doesn't stink and one day she is going to learn otherwise."

"I wish the two of you would try to get along. She's my best friend and you're my man. I don't want to be caught in the middle."

"And I don't like her putting crazy ideas into your pretty head. I like the way things have gone with us these last few months, and I just don't want anyone to destroy that."

"Oh, really now?" I asked as Drake planted a kiss, then another, on my neck. He knew that was one of my weak spots; the meltdown began.

"Definitely. I like how you let me order for you in restaurants, how you accept my advice and opinions, surrender to me in the bedroom. Just small things like that."

"Do you?" I asked while he traced a line up my arm.

"Yes, Miss Logan, I do." Drake tweaked a nipple between his thumb and forefinger.

I moaned passionately. "And a woman shouldn't be vocal and proactive in achieving her goals?"

"I'm not saying that. I'm simply stating that a real woman should make an effort to please her man and take care of his needs. If I tell you to get down on your knees and suck my dick, I expect you to do it. No questions asked. Again, there can only be one leader in a relationship. That's why Taylor can't keep a man; she thinks she's one."

"You are sounding like a male chauvinist, babe."

For a moment, an angry look crossed Drake's face and just as quickly disappeared. Then he broke into a huge, mischievous smile and he reached for me.

"Call it what you want. Now come here and surrender to your man again," he said, as his hand found the warm place between my legs. "Dance for me."

"What? Dance for you? Are you serious?"

"Stop with all the questions. Don't I look serious? Stand up and do a striptease for me."

"No, I don't think so," I said, embarrassed at the thought.

"Come on, just a small one," he said, tugging on my arm to pull me to a standing position.

"I don't know," I said, pulling the sheet tighter around me.

"I thought you loved me."

"I do, babe."

"Well then, do this for me. Kennedy, it's just you and me here. We are behind closed doors."

"Okay, but just a little one," I said, motioning with my finger.

"Just a little one then, "Drake said softly, assaulting my neck with kisses.

I hesitated.

"Okay, let's see what you got," he said, placing his hands behind his head and leaning back against his pillow, waiting for the show to begin. I shyly released the sheet and stood up in all my naked glory. Slowly, I started moving around doing a belly dancer–type routine that I saw on TV at some point. Drake was taking it all in like he was watching a show.

"That's it. Lower your hands so I can see those gorgeous tatas. You know I'm a breast man."

I continued to dance as I slowly lowered my hands, then raised them above my head, twirling my fingers in midair.

"Yeah, nice. Turn around, slowly. Tease me . . . Not too fast. Now, touch yourself for me, baby."

"No."

"Touch yourself. Don't be shy. Play with your breasts and nipples. Real slow. We got all night."

I paused for just a moment. Drake's lust-filled eyes never left mine and I obliged.

"Yeah, squeeze your nipple. A little harder. The other one. Harder. Make 'em stand at attention for your man. Salute me."

"Drake?"

"Shhh, you're doing great. Now, keep one hand on your breast and move your other hand down between your thighs."

"I don't know."

"Come on. Right now, you are sexy as hell. You got my dick hard as bricks . . . That's right. Don't stop; touch yourself. Stick two fingers in. Deeper. Pull 'em out. Back in. In. Out.

"Look at you. Yeah, you're getting good and wet for me. Yes, I love it.

"Moan for me. Let me hear you enjoying yourself. That turns me on.

"Keep stroking. Stick your finger all the way in. Faster. Open your legs wider and bend your knees.

With my eyes closed, head thrown back, my breathing was getting more erratic by the minute.

"That's my girl. Get yourself off. Get yours before I get up in there. Come here, let me taste you," he said, sticking my fingers in his mouth and sucking. "Hmm, finger lickin' good. Delicious. Come here," he said again, this time pulling me down onto the bed, on top of him.

Drake entered me quickly and roughly, a squeal of surprise escaping me. Tonight we weren't making love; tonight was fuck night. We had those too, just like costume night. Drake was going to fuck me unmercifully as he frantically gripped and maneuvered my hips up and down to the steady, rhythmic beat of his relentless dick. With every thrust of his rod, my womanhood eagerly anticipated and accepted the next one, pulling him in.

Later, still not sated, he smacked my butt as he leaned me over a chair and entered me from behind, pulling my torso into him as he bit down on my neck and gave me every inch he had. Over and over he stroked.

"Work that ass. Take this dick. Open that pussy up for me. That's right." He pushed my legs open with his knees and smacked my ass.

"Ohhh. Ahhh. Ohhh. Yeah. You like this dick, don't you? Don't you?" he asked, smacking my ass again.

"Ohhh, yes, babe."

"You ready to come? You almost there?"

"Ohhh. Yeah."

"Come on my dick."

"Ohhh. Ohhh. Oh . . . my . . . God."

"Yeah, this is mine. My pussy."

Chapter 15

"Mrs. Logan, thanks again for inviting me. Dinner was delicious. I eat out so often that a home-cooked meal is a real treat," Taylor cited, stretching on the sofa and making herself right at home. She was there for moral support.

"You are quite welcome, dear. A friend of Kennedy is always welcomed with open arms. I love you like a second daughter, I'll pack you a plate to take home before you leave."

Taylor and I exchanged quick, secretive glances. We had moved into the living room after literally stuffing ourselves with Mother's smothered pork chops and gravy, brown rice, and collards. We drank a pitcher of lemonade among us. I was very pleased that my appetite had returned and I was even gaining a little weight. I saw that as one of the first steps toward getting my life back.

"Thank you. I appreciate that," Taylor said, smiling in Mother's direction.

"I hope you will look out for Kennedy when I move back home."

"Mother. I'm a grown woman. I don't need Taylor watching over me. I'm sure Taylor has more exciting things to do with her time than babysit me. And besides, you're only moving across town."

"Child, haven't you learned? Everybody needs some-body," Mother scolded.

"Don't worry, Mrs. Logan. I'll be happy to make sure Kennedy eats right and doesn't wear herself out," Taylor cooed sweetly.

I rolled my eyes at Taylor as Mother rose from her chair and walked into the kitchen to wash and put away the dinner dishes. Even though I had a perfectly new dishwasher that came with the apartment, she refused to use it.

When Mother was out of hearing range, Taylor whis-pered, "Well, are you going to tell her?"

"Yeah. Give me a minute."

"You didn't mention it throughout the entire dinner. I thought that was the grand plan we discussed. You were going to tell her about your daddy's girlfriend walking out on him and about your search for your birth mom."

"I'm waiting for the right moment."

"K, it's never going to be the exact right moment. Just tell her," Taylor whispered back. "I have your back."

I'd asked Taylor to support me in my decision to search for my birth mom by being by my side when I informed Mother of my plan. I wasn't sure how Mother would react, but this was something I had to do. I had pondered long and hard about finding her over the last year. When I was younger, I never thought I'd want to meet my birth mom, but I had always felt a piece of myself was missing. As much as I loved Mother and Daddy, I still longed to know my original roots. I think everyone has an innate desire to know where they came from.

Almost a year ago, after watching an episode on a talk show, I felt more and more compelled to follow through on my search. One of the guests was a middle-aged woman who was reunited with her birth mom after forty years of separation. It was a true tearjerker. There wasn't a dry eye in the studio audience or on me.

However, I didn't want Mother to think that my search for my biological mom made me love her any less. I just wanted answers from my birth mom, that's all. Nothing more, nothing less. Maybe by understanding her, I could determine why I had made some of the bad decisions I had in my life. Maybe it could help explain why I drew toxic relationships into my life.

I also hadn't told Mother about Daddy's present situation yet. I figured I'd tackle that task first. To be honest, I wasn't sure how she'd react about that either. On a small level, I'm sure she would gloat. Daddy left Mother for a younger woman and now that younger woman had left him for someone. Used him and left him, high and dry. I'm positive that tidbit of information would give Mother some form of satisfaction, and an "I told you so" was somewhere in that equation. I wasn't sure if she'd want to speak with him, though. On the surface, she appeared to despise the man. Deep down, I think she still loved him with everything she had.

Taylor was still stretched out on the sofa, making herself at home while she flipped through magazines that were spread out neatly on the coffee table. My entire apartment was spotless. Mother had cleaned up from top to bottom and had even gone grocery shopping. I had a week's supply of cooked and frozen meals in my freezer. And she washed and dried my clothes.

"Mother, you sure you don't need any help?" I shouted into the kitchen.

"No. You and Taylor entertain yourselves. I'm just fine, don't worry about me."

I knew she wouldn't ask for any help. She was still spoiling me and treating me as an invalid. However, I'd have my home back by tonight. I was ashamed to say I was extremely happy.

"Mother, guess who I spoke with a few days ago?"

"I don't know. Who?" she asked, distracted.

"You're not going to guess?" I asked, stalling for time.

"Kennedy?"

"I talked with Daddy."

Silence followed. Taylor kept her head buried in the magazine.

Finally, she responded. "Good for you, dear."

"Daddy said to tell you hello and asked how you were doing."

"Ump."

"And he said he needs to talk with you about something."

"About what?" she asked, peeking her head around the corner. Curiosity had gotten the best of her.

"I'm just giving you his message. I don't know; he didn't tell me," I lied.

"Honestly, it really doesn't matter. We have nothing to discuss. He made his choice years ago, now he has to live with that," she said, walking back into the kitchen to dry the dishes.

"I think that's what he wants to discuss."

Out of the corner of my eye, I saw Mother dry off her hands with a dishcloth, place it on the stove rack, and slowly walk back into the living room.

It's now or never.

Taylor pretended to be totally engrossed in an article in *Today's Black Woman*. I knew it. She wasn't going to be any help besides moral support.

By now, Mother had trekked the short distance back into the living room. I had her full, undivided attention. "Kennedy, what are you talking about? Stop speaking in riddles. First you say you don't know, and then you say you do. What does your father want to discuss?"

"You really should talk to him."

"I've already told you, I have nothing to discuss with that old fool. I should have listened to my parents years ago and never married him."

"Well, I don't know, Mother. This really isn't my business; I should let Daddy tell you."

"Tell me what? You've gone this far, you might as well spill the rest." Mother stood there and glared down expectantly at me; she stood her ground and wasn't going anywhere without answers to her questions.

Internally, I debated back and forth if I should render the news. However, with her nosey self, I knew it would kill her if she didn't find out what I was talking about. She probably wouldn't even go home and that certainly was not happening.

"I'll tell you," I stated swiftly.

"I'm waiting," she said, silently tapping her right foot with her left hand propped on her hip. I looked to Taylor for help; she was totally into that magazine.

"Loretta left Daddy."

"She what?"

"Loretta left Daddy a few weeks ago."

I saw the beginnings of a smile forming on Mother's

lips, but she quickly tried, unsuccessfully, to bring it under control.

"Serves him right. Old geezer thinking he can handle a young thing like that home wrecker. She is nothing but a she-devil in disguise."

I remained silent. I didn't comment one way or another.

"What does he want from me? I know he doesn't think he can come crawling back to me now that that Jezebel has tossed him away like yesterday's garbage. Serves him right," she gloated.

"He just asked me to deliver his message. And I've done that."

"Ump. I've moved on. I have a very nice gentleman friend," Mother cited to herself more than to me. "He treats me just fine and appreciates a mature woman."

Taylor looked up once, smiled at Mother, and immediately looked back down at the magazine. I wanted to strangle her. Some help she turned out to be.

"I guess that hussy got tired of waiting for his Viagra to kick in. Probably got herself a young stud that didn't need the stuff; his worked just fine. I was lucky if your daddy could handle one round of lovemaking."

"Mother, I don't know and I really don't need to know all the personal details," I gushed as I caught Taylor, out of the corner of my eye, trying to hold back a giggle. I blushed.

"See, Taylor, that's what I like about you. Always have. You don't let your world revolve around one man."

"Ma'am?" she questioned, finally looking up for longer than five seconds.

"You don't give your heart away to the first man

who comes along with sweet words and promises. You know who you are and you're comfortable in your own skin. I admit, I've learned the hard way, but I'm still trying to make Kennedy understand that in order to love we don't have to become something we aren't. We don't have to lose ourselves in the process."

With those comments, Mother excused herself, turned, and headed into her bedroom to finish packing her last few items. Boxes were all over the place. I hadn't realized how much stuff she had accumulated during her stay.

"I think that went well," Taylor laughed, smiling my way. I simply rolled my eyes at her.

"That was strange. Even though she was gloating and happy that Daddy and Loretta's relationship ended, she still found a way to flip it in our direction."

"And speaking of that, what have you been telling your mom about me?"

"Nothing. You know I don't gossip with Mother like that. She did seem to have you pegged though. I guess she calls them as she sees them." I giggled. This time Taylor did the eye rolling.

"Don't laugh, K. She had your number too. And you didn't even have the opportunity to tell her about your search for your birth mom."

"I know," I stated, looking disappointed.

"Maybe today wasn't a good time anyway. She has had enough news for one day."

"Yeah, I think you're right," I said, sitting in the love seat across from the sofa.

"Have you started yet?"

"Started what?"

"Your search, silly," Taylor said.

"Sorta. I've registered with a couple of agencies and given them all the information I've been told over the years, which isn't much. Maybe this isn't a good idea after all and I should drop it."

"K, don't look so down and give up before you even begin. Personally, I think you should pursue it. I'll ask around and see if I can get a referral for an agency too."

I remained silent.

"We've discussed this, K. You deserve to have some answers. You're just feeling anxious right now."

"That I am."

"Whether your mom realizes it or not, she does too."

"What?"

"Deserves some answers. She should talk to your dad."

By eight o'clock that night, Taylor and I had successfully moved Mother back home, safe and sound. After receiving a stern lecture and more unsolicited advice before leaving her house, I was finally behind closed doors at my own place. After wrapping up some containers of leftovers, Taylor left.

It felt funny not having Mother at my apartment; it was downright lonely and suddenly too quiet. I hadn't realized I had gotten so used to her constant chatter and presence. Now, there was just silence. Silence that gave me an opportunity to think, reflect, and remember. Of course, Drake was the main focus. Finding my birth mom came in a close second. I had never realized how badly I wanted to connect with her until I made the decision to search for her.

By nine o'clock, I had my music blasting as I strolled around buck-naked, lighting candles throughout the place. Silence is not always golden.

Chapter 16

Monday morning came before I knew it, or was ready for it. I absolutely hate Monday mornings. They are a constant reminder that I'm a slave to corporate America for at least the next five days. Ugh.

I awoke sweaty and tangled in my sheets, with my comforter on the floor. I had tossed and turned all night in my lonely apartment. Every sound was elevated tenfold. I witnessed every creak and groan of the walls settling. I heard my upstairs neighbor when he arrived home and attended to various household duties. I swear the man is a night owl, or vampire. Who vacuums at ten at night? Faintly, I could even pick up traffic sounds two streets over, on a major bypass.

Around six o'clock A.M., just as I was finally dosing off into a deep, restless sleep, the alarm clock blared me awake. I lay there for another ten minutes, unable to move the few feet to the bathroom to begin my day.

I felt horrible and I didn't look any better with the heavy, puffy bags concentrated under my eyes. I didn't feel like going into work, but if I didn't I knew I'd mope around the apartment all day. For some reason, I was afraid to be alone with my random thoughts. So, off to work I went, grumpy and all. If I had known what was coming, I would have stayed at home, in bed.

***

Around nine o'clock, after I'd finished off my first can of soda, I had a surge of energy. I could feel the caffeine and sugar surging through my veins, giving me an instant high. It gave me renewed energy to tackle the massive e-mails in my inbox. In need of a diversion from my issues, I dove in.

At ten o'clock, my manager informed me that there was an emergency meeting upstairs that I was to attend in her absence. She had another client meeting that couldn't be missed, and since she couldn't be in two places at once, I was her stand-in. My stomach immediately fell to my knees because I knew Drake would be a part of the mandatory meeting. I'd have to be in the same room with him for at least an hour or more. That realization frightened me and made me sick to my stomach.

At first, I debated faking illness and leaving for the day, but I couldn't run from him forever. Besides, my manager believed in me and confirmed I was an asset by sending me to represent our department at an important meeting. Today was the day I'd make a stand and prove I was strong. Drake wanted me to bow down and surrender. I refused.

I arrived upstairs ten minutes before the meeting was to begin. I figured I'd need the additional minutes to pull myself together and psych myself up. Plus, I needed to review the agenda. A friendly administrative assistant informed me in which conference room the meeting was to be held. I was one of the first to arrive in the large conference room at the end of the hallway. I spoke to the two other women who were already there and made sure I secured a seat near the middle of the table. I didn't want to be up front, where I knew Drake would be. Yet, I didn't want to entirely disappear at the very back, either.

Slowly, different managers starting drifting in with cups of freshly brewed coffee and pen and notepads in hand. Drake was one of the last to arrive. For just a quick second, I saw the surprise flash across his face when he saw me seated at the massive table. I looked down at my yellow legal pad and pretended to read my briefing. As always, his presence intoxicated and over-whelmed me.

"Okay, people, let's go ahead and get this meeting started," Drake said, chairing the meeting and look-ing from one to the other of us. "We all have a lot on our plates today, and I apologize for taking you away from other matters. However, we have a small crisis on our hands that needs to be addressed and handled as promptly as possible."

He stood tall and confident as he went on to inform us that several of our major clients were threatening to pull out once their contracts ended in a couple of months. Their company bigwigs had complaints of in-ferior service and poor customer service, among other things, and said they could obtain lower pricing struc-tures elsewhere.

They had been clients for many, many years and brought in an enormous amount of revenue. Everyone seated at the table knew there was no way in hell we could afford to lose them. We had to handle them with kid gloves and come up with a planned resolution; our jobs depended upon it.

Drake skillfully went over the history of our clients, revenue figures, and then addressed each complaint. When he came to the customer service piece, he looked directly at me for guidance.

"It appears we have Miss Logan in our presence today. For those of you who don't know her, she's a senior RSR and very familiar with these particular clients. Maybe she can be so kind as to address some of these issues concerning customer service." Then he looked at me again and smiled, knowing he had put me on the spot. I wasn't prepared. I was simply sitting in for my manager. He knew that.

All eyes turned in my direction for clarification and understanding. I felt my face flushing. I swallowed the lump in my throat and gulped.

"Mr. Collins, this is the first time that I've been made aware of these complaints concerning our department. As you know, I'm sitting in for my manager who had a conflicting appointment. I'll be happy to tag this as a take-away item, investigate, and report back to everyone ASAP."

Drake sat there with a big smirk on his face. I wanted to slap it off. Honestly, I just wanted to slap him, period. "Miss Logan, as you know, this is of a most urgent nature. Time is of the utmost importance. Can you shed any light at all on the current situation? And when can we expect to receive your report?"

"Today, by five o'clock."

Not trying to shift blame, I proceeded to explain what I knew of the situation, starting with high turnover ratios in our department contributing to unusually heavy workloads. Until very recently, multiple reps had handled the clients' accounts.

"Very good. Thank you, Miss Logan, for your input," Drake stated, as his eyes eagerly took me in. "I'll expect to have that report, in more detail, by five o'clock sharp. Please copy everyone in this room as well."

"Thank you, Mr. Collins," I responded. I was pleased with my comeback in his effort to make me look incompetent in front of my colleagues.

"Unless there are any more questions or concerns, I suggest we all get back to work, and with your take-aways in hand, be prepared to meet again on Wednesday, same time and place. I'll have my administrative assistant send out an agenda. Thank you."

Everyone rose to leave, chatting among themselves. "Miss Logan, may I speak with you for a minute, please?"

I wanted to scream out, "Hell no," but controlled myself.

"Sure," was all I said. Drake was now seated at the head of the table. He hadn't looked up again and was reading his notes. By now, mostly everyone had filtered out the room into the hallway.

"Do you mind closing the door, Miss Logan, so that we may speak privately?"

As I got up to close the door, I could feel his eyes taking me in. Caressing my body. At one time, I enjoyed knowing that my man was watching me. Now, it made my skin crawl. I stopped myself from scratching. Fearing the conversation, I turned slowly around, didn't make eye contact, and sat two seats down from him.

"You did great today. I put you on the spot intentionally, but you were quick on your feet. I respect the way you didn't tolerate everyone placing full blame on your department for the mess we are in. You were very loyal."

"Loyal to those who deserve it."

Drake calmly laughed and stared at me for a few seconds.

"You look very nice today."

"What do you need to speak with me about?"

"Oh, so now you don't have any manners? You look very nice today," he repeated.

"Thank you."

Drake reached for my hand. "I've missed you, Kennedy. I can't get you out of my head."

I pulled my hand from his reach. "Is that all, Mr. Collins?" I acted as if I hadn't heard his previous comment.

"Did you hear me?"

"Yes, I certainly did. Is that all?"

"Wow. This is a different side of you. I'm not used to all this feistiness coming from you."

Drake chose that moment to move and sit directly next to me. I instantly felt a powerful combination of uneasiness and desire rise from the pit of my stomach. Despite my negative feelings for him, he was still a very handsome and sexy man. No one could take that away from him. And today, dressed in a black suit with a crisp white shirt, his hair freshly cut and smelling divine, I couldn't help but notice and wonder how he could look so good on the outside and be so messed up on the inside.

"You are so beautiful. You're all I think about lately. When are you going to forgive me and let bygones be bygones?" He reached over and caressed my face and hair.

I froze.

I couldn't believe what he was saying. Let bygones be bygones. Like we had had a simple argument over something trivial. He was either in denial, or totally insane; maybe both.

"How about never? Is that clear enough?"

"You can't mean that. I promise, what happened will never happen again. It was a test."

"If that's all, I have to get back to my desk. I have a report to deliver by five. Sharp." I stood to leave.

He roughly grabbed my arm and pushed me back down into the chair. "This meeting isn't over. I am your superior, Kennedy, and don't you forget that. I can make your life a living hell. With the economy the way it is, now isn't a good time to search for a new job. Do you understand me?"

I didn't respond, partly because I was in shock.

Drake then reached down, boldly placed his large hand inside my blouse and fondled my left breast, first gently, then more roughly as I attempted to pull away.

"What are you doing? Take your hands off me," I screamed through gritted teeth.

Drake grabbed me by the wrist. "We'll continue this conversation later, Kennedy."

"Don't hold your breath."

"Good day, Miss Logan. We'll talk later. Real soon, away from here."

"Stay away from me. I mean it, or—"

"Or you'll what? Go to your manager, who is seriously sweating me by the way, and tell her that I've been fucking you silly and that you've loved every damn minute of it? I don't think so."

I looked at him in utter disbelief, not moving. Frozen in time.

"Kennedy, you don't air your dirty laundry like that. You're too much of a lady. Well, that's what everyone thinks anyway. I've seen the real Kennedy. The real freak."

"Stop," I screamed, placing my hands over my ears to block out his words.

"Kennedy, you should know by now that I get what I want, one way or the other. And I want you. And I will have you," Drake stated, tracing a circle around my nipple through the sheer silk of my blouse.

I slapped his hand away. "Why are you doing this to me?" I cried.

"Because I can and I haven't given up on us."

"You're sick." I shook my head sadly. "I can't believe I thought I loved you. You don't even know the meaning of the word. How could I have been so blind? So misled?"

"At some point in time, y'all all do . . . think you love me. Women always confuse a good fuck with love. I, on the other hand, know that good pussy is just that: good pussy. Nothing more, nothing less. Fix yourself up and get back to work."

With that, Drake turned and readied himself to walk out of the room. Not another word was spoken, but the tension in the air could slice through steel.

After I had composed myself enough to walk out of the conference room, I found the administrative assistant sitting at her desk, looking at me curiously. I turned away and kept walking. As I stifled a sniffle, I could feel her questioning eyes boring into my back.

Chapter 17

Dear Journal,

It's after midnight and I can't sleep. Again. I know I have work in the morning and will be sluggish all day, but for now, I can't sleep. After the scene in the conference room with Drake, I'm wound up too tight. I feel like a jack in the box before it springs. I've got to figure out what to do about Drake. Now he has thrown sexual harassment into the mix. The layers of drama get thicker and thicker. How dare he put his hands on me? My instincts told me it was a mistake to start a relationship with him. Now I don't know which way to turn.

Earlier, Mother called to check on me. I'm completely surprised that she hadn't called sooner. She hinted around about Drake, but didn't come right out and ask me anything direct. I knew all she sought and needed was confirmation that he was out of my life for good. She and Taylor were much alike in that they shared their intense dislike for Drake.

Now I am sitting with a steaming cup of green tea cupped between my hands and my journal propped up on my lap. As the tea relaxes me and my mind wanders back in time, I realize that

Drake gave off clear signals from the very beginning that he wasn't all he made himself out to be. I guess there are always signs if you are observant and watchful. A person, in time, will show you who they are. It's true: If it sounds (in his case, looks) too good to be true, it probably is. Unfortunately, I refused to see the signs and was too much in love to care, until it was too late.

In the beginning, Drake treated me like a princess, his special princess, and he was my prince. We managed to keep our relationship under wraps at work and that made it even more thrilling. Passing each other in the lobby of our building or riding up in the elevator together, sometimes attending the same meetings . . . It was exciting to know we had been intimate and no one else knew. That was our little secret. I secretly smiled inside at the comments I overheard about Drake. He was the object of many of my coworkers' fantasies. If they only knew that we shared a bed and all the things that they pictured him doing to them, he was doing to me.

Outside of work, Drake literally wined and dined me all across the city; we shared many expensive, intimate, and romantic dinners. Drake spoiled me with extravagant presents for no apparent reason. He always stated that if I was on his arm, I had to look like a million dollars.

Drake surprised me with spur-of-the-moment weekend trips and, of course, he took me to new levels in the bedroom. What more could a girl ask for? I had no complaints. I overlooked the fact that he sometimes tried to bully me into being more aggressive on personal and professional levels. Drake had an innate ability of picking up on a person's weakness and running with it.

In our early months together, we were rarely apart from one another on the weekends. Occasionally, he'd fly home for a long weekend to visit his family or handle personal matters back in Los Angeles. He never went into detail about the personal matters and I never meddled. Even though Drake talked about his family, I still had never met any of them. I really didn't think anything about it. I talked briefly to his mom and she was pleasant enough. I knew, in time, I would have the opportunity to fly to Los Angeles and meet them because I saw a clear future with this man.

I admit, sometimes I saw a darker side. I noticed but chose to ignore how he'd talk down to waitresses or waiters if everything wasn't just right to his specifications at a restaurant. Sure, you should complain if something isn't right with your food or the service, but Drake would be downright brutal with his comments. I noticed how he'd treat a hotel employee like they were several notches beneath him. The maids were treated like his personal servants who were placed in the hotel to service him and his immediate needs.

I'd heard the story of how, before he met me, he stayed at a five-star hotel in Chicago and had gotten all hot and bothered from watching a steamy show on cable TV. He had called downstairs and complained about the minibar not being fully

*stocked or the lack of fresh towels in the bath-
room; I can't remember. The housekeeping staff
had sent a housekeeper up right away: a pretty,
buxom Mexican woman.*

*Drake bragged about how, after just a little
convincing, in the limited Spanish he knew, he
paid her twenty-five dollars with a five-dollar tip
to perform oral sex on him. She'd gotten down
on her knees, unbuttoned the top of her uniform
so that he could fondle her large breasts, and
senorita went to work on him. Sucked him bone
dry while he sat in a chair and played with her
breasts. Afterward, she pulled back his covers
and placed a mint on his pillow. Drake found
great humor in sharing that adventure. It disturbed me for days.*

*Again, I heard and saw other signs. Love can
make us act in ways that are unnatural to our
very being. I remember the first time he focused
his anger on me. Now, that was a different story.
Suddenly, I took notice. One Friday evening, we
had made plans to attend a party that one of his
clients was hosting and had invited him and a
guest to attend. It was an annual black tie affair.
Drake gave me his credit card and told me to go
out and shop for a sexy evening gown. He wanted
all the men at the party to be drooling over me on
his arm.*

*I did as he said, went out to Lenox Mall and
purchased a gorgeous designer, sexy black evening gown. I even splurged on new shoes, an
evening bag, matching accessories, and sexy lingerie. I knew what the end of the evening held in
store for us.*

I took my time and put in extra effort to get dressed that night; I had gotten a manicure and spa pedicure. My hair and makeup were perfect; I thought I was looking great. When Drake arrived at my door, his eyes told a different story.

"Hey, babe," I said, planting a kiss on his lips and pulling him in from the doorway.

"You look so handsome," I stated, admiring him in his tux. "Give me one second. I need to grab my wrap off the bed."

It did not go unnoticed that Drake still hadn't spoken.

"Wait. Come here, Kennedy," he commanded, pulling me back to him roughly by my shoulders.

"Ouch. What?"

"What is this?" he asked, looking me up and down with disdain.

"You like?" I asked, thinking I was looking like Miss Diva as I swirled around and around for him to take me in from every angle.

"I thought I told you to buy something sexy."

"I did. I'm wearing what your money purchased," I said slowly as confusion registered on my face.

"You've got to be kidding."

"I'm not. What's wrong with this?" I cried, looking down at myself.

"That shit looks like something my mother would wear. Well, actually, my mother wouldn't even wear that."

"I know you aren't serious," I cried as big tears crept down my face.

"I'm very serious, Kennedy. I'm very disappointed as well. I don't ask much from you and you can't even get that right."

"Drake, this is my definition of sexy. Very classy. I didn't think you wanted me looking like a slut."

Drake didn't respond. I dropped my head because I didn't want him to see my tears.

"I can change. Put on something. . . ." I stated, walking toward my bedroom.

"No. We don't have time. Let's just go," he screamed, walking ahead of me and out the front door. By the time I locked my door, he was waiting in the car. He didn't even bother to get out and open my door. Drake sat behind the wheel and sulked like a baby, looking straight ahead. He wouldn't even look at me.

The ride to the event was driven in complete silence. You would have thought I had committed a violent crime against him or something. Drake was steaming. I had never seen him that agitated. And at me. I would soon learn that if Drake didn't get his way, there would be hell to pay. I wasn't really paying attention to where we were going. All I knew was that the event was hosted at a hotel in Midtown and I was still trying to figure out exactly what was wrong with my outfit. When Drake pulled up into a popular gentlemen's club, I came back to my senses and checked out my surroundings.

"Why are we stopping here?" I questioned, looking around. Loud music could be heard all the way in the parking lot. Drake stared straight ahead. I could see his jaw muscles flinching up and down as he attempted to maintain his composure.

"Just follow me," he stated, coming around and opening my car door. As he helped me out, pulling me roughly by the elbow, he still hadn't looked directly at me as he reached for my hand.

"What about the party?"

Drake dropped my hand, stopped, and gave me a look to kill. *"Forget the party. I'm going to show you what sexy is. Put it in your pretty little head: when I tell my woman to dress sexy, next time you'd better follow my instructions. Understand?"*

I didn't say anything.

"I said do you understand?"

I nodded. *"Drake, I don't want to go in there. Are you crazy?"*

"Come on, Kennedy," he stated, taking my hand again and leading the way, literally half dragging me along.

"Look at how we're dressed. We'll stand out like a sore thumb. Everyone will be staring at us."

"I don't care. Quit worrying about what someone thinks of you. That's your damn problem. Quit giving a shit about what everyone thinks of you. Live for yourself."

I hesitated, still uncertain.

"Let's go. I'm not going to tell you again." He firmly gripped my wrist until it was painful.

I followed him in. For the rest of the night as he drank and watched the adult entertainment, I sat quietly by his side. I soon realized Drake was not a stranger to the club. Several of the waitresses and dancers spoke to him and called him by name.

Now and then, he'd point out one of the dancers who he thought was really hot and sexy. He'd hold up a few dollar bills and they'd dance over for an up-close-and-personal performance. Two hours later, Drake had pulled off his jacket, unbuttoned his shirt collar, had downed three drinks, and had the strippers, the ones with the big breasts, giving him lap dances.

I shrunk further and further into my seat. I wanted to disappear. Half the time, Drake acted like I wasn't even there anyway. He was so into the dancers that he totally ignored me; barely spoke to me. He was too busy copping feels and getting tatas rubbed across his face. I had never felt more humiliated in my entire life.

When I arrived home that night, I was so disgusted with myself and mainly with Drake. Why hadn't I said something? Why didn't I demand that he show me respect and take me home? I just sat there and let him embarrass and humiliate me in front of a room full of patrons. I didn't invite him in to my apartment. And now, come to think of it, he didn't ask. I took a long, hot shower after tossing the dreaded dress in the trashcan. I felt a need to wash away all the filth I had witnessed that evening. Drake included.

I was totally confused. I'd never seen that side of Drake before. At work, he was the ultimate professional. Up until that point, he had been the perfect boyfriend and lover. What happened? Was he showing his true colors now that he was comfortable with me, or was this a brief lapse in judgment?

I cried myself to sleep and pretty much tossed and turned all night. My dreams were filled with images of dancing girls who giggled and cooed and jumped to Drake's every command. I knew in my heart I couldn't continue a relationship in which I was disrespected. I didn't have long to reflect on a decision.

The next morning, I received two dozen long-stemmed red roses, an invitation to brunch, and a heartfelt apology. Drake explained that he was under so much pressure at work and he wanted to make a good impression on his client by showing up with a sexy, gorgeous woman on his arm. Evidently, his client had a reputation as a ladies' man and appreciated a beautiful woman. Because I didn't want to lose him, I eagerly accepted his apology and explanation. All was good in my world again because Drake was still in it. Little did I know, this was just the beginning of a series of emotional abuses and breakups.

Chapter 18

"Hello?"

No response was heard.

"Uh. Uh, hello?

Deadly, total silence. You could hear a pin drop.

"Hello? I know you're there. How are you, dear? It's been awhile."

"I know this isn't who I think it is," Dorothy Logan whispered into the phone, clutching it with all her might.

"Yes, it's Robert."

"Robert?"

"Yes, your ex-husband. Please don't hang up."

"Kennedy informed me that you wanted to talk, but I didn't think you'd actually have the audacity to pick up the phone, dial my number, and face me like a man. Not after all this time."

"Dorothy, please. Let's not start arguing. This is hard enough for me as it is."

"Robert Logan, don't you tell me what to do. You hear me? Don't start with me. You don't have that right. You threw that right out, along with thirty years of marriage. Just like throwing out the bathwater. And let's not talk about what is hard for you. I don't give a damn. What about me? It hasn't been smooth sailing for me either."

"You're right. Absolutely right. About everything."

There was another long moment of silence. Awkward strained seconds that passed by in slow, strained motion. Both Dorothy and Robert were thinking of better times. Times when conversation wasn't forced, or filled with angry words and even harsher realities.

Again, Robert broke the reflection.

"I'm not going to beat around the bush, so let me come out with it. Loretta left me. Packed her bags, waltzed out the door, and never looked back, not once."

"Ump."

"I know Kennedy told you because you got that child trained to be both your eyes and ears."

"Good. Serves you right. I'm glad she left your ass. Old fool trying to hang with a young fool. So now, who's the bigger one?"

Robert knew this thrashing was coming and he accepted it like a man. Sucked it up. Actually, he knew it was long overdue. Five years ago, so many words were left unspoken. There was never real closure.

"For your information, that child worships the ground you walk on. Kennedy stays out of our business; has from the very beginning. She doesn't want to take sides and hurt you or me," Dorothy stated. "Tell me, why are you calling to tell me that hussy left you?"

"I feel like I owe you that because her leaving made me stop and think."

"Ump. You haven't thought in five years."

"I deserved that. I've lost so much; given up so much. I hurt so many people in the process. But you're right, I didn't know what I was thinking," Robert shared.

"I don't either. You gave up all our years together to run off with a woman twenty years your junior. We had a lot of history together, decades. Most of it was good.

I thought we'd built a solid life together; I thought we were happy. We had beat the odds that my parents said were against us. What got into you?"

"You're so right, Dorothy. Hindsight is twenty/twenty. There's much to be said about thinking the grass is greener on the other side."

"Will you stop saying I'm so right?"

"I can't argue with you about anything you're saying. It's all true. And now, you can gloat and tell me you told me so as many times as you please, if that makes you happy."

"I haven't been truly happy in a long time, Robert, and your misfortune doesn't bring me joy. I'm a good Christian. I used to think it would, but now I just don't care. I'll pray for you. Is that all, Robert?"

"I just wanted to talk; hear your voice. Say I'm sorry, I apologize. Now, I see what my leaving must have felt like for you. We do reap what we sow. I'm truly sorry, Dorothy, for any pain or sorrow that I sent your way. I hope that one day you'll find it in your heart to forgive me. That's all I wanted to say. I know it's a little late, but it's from the heart."

Another tense moment of uncomfortable silence passed like the sand in an hourglass. Dorothy had a moment of clarity and realized what was done was done. Water under the bridge. They couldn't change the past, or go back and rewind the hands of time. And really, she had gotten what she wanted all these years: an apology. There were still many questions to be asked and many answers to be heard, but she had gotten her much-needed and desired apology.

"I accept it and I forgive you, Robert."

"Thank you. You don't know what a relief that is,

to know that you truly forgive me, " he cried into the phone.

"I forgive you, but I'll never forget. Fools forget and I'm not a fool."

"I can accept that; I have no choice."

"How are you doing, Robert? Really?"

"Living. I'm hanging in here. I've seen better days, but I'm old and wise enough to count my daily blessings. What about you?"

"About the same. Just living and looking to better days. I can't ask for more. I'm blessed to have my health and strength."

"Dorothy, regardless of all that happened between us, I never stopped loving you. I mean that sincerely from the bottom of my heart. You will always hold a special place there. No one can replace that."

Dorothy laughed a tired, weary laugh. "Well, you have a funny way of showing it, old man."

"See, you hit the nail on the head. I felt like an old man when I was with you and I was terrified of living my last days just waiting to die."

"What? What are you talking about? I never knew you felt like that."

"Of course you didn't. You never asked. You had a tendency to talk and not listen. You heard what you needed to hear. Loretta, she brought excitement and a new zest for life my way. She made me feel young and vibrant."

"I don't care to hear about that home wrecker. But, you have many more productive years before you leave this earth."

"I hope so, God willing, but I felt like I was missing something. I needed some excitement, something different from our day-to-day existence. I know you don't understand, but—"

"I do, Robert. I'm human. Sometimes, I have the same feelings. I dream of vacationing in Europe and traveling the world. And by the way, I never stopped loving you. I just placed it somewhere where I couldn't feel it."

The next two hours were spent on catching up with each other's lives and obtaining the answers to many unanswered, lingering questions. Barriers, anger, and resentment were slowly crumbling away, chip by chip. Bit by bit.

Chapter 19

Dear Journal,
As more and more time went by, I found myself changing. Changing to fit what Drake wanted me to be. Normally, I was more reserved, laid-back, and not really a party person. Drake loved being the center of attention and adored being the life of the party. Such differences in personality traits should have told me we were incompatible. However, I was under the illusion that opposites attract. Plus, Drake was hinting that I was exactly the type of woman he wanted as a wife, lover, and confidante. I immediately had images of our perfect family: the babies, white picket fence, minivan, and an almost perfect, adoring, and loving husband.

My transformation to please the man I loved was gradual. Nothing major. Just minor things. A change here. Something different there. An action that was out of my norm. Yet, they all added up to what Drake desired. His idea of a perfect woman. I stopped drinking sodas. I started drinking alcohol more socially. I began to dress sexier. We started going out to clubs instead of spending quiet nights at home or going to a good movie or play.

I started doing what Drake told me to do. If he told me not to cut my hair, I didn't cut my hair. If he wanted me to get a bikini wax, I got one. If I made plans with Taylor or Mother and Drake wanted to spend time with me, I cancelled my previous commitments with no hesitation, even at a moment's notice. I tried things sexually that I'd never done with previous lovers. Soon, that became a problem. A major one.

Chapter 20

Traffic in Atlanta was horrific. Even driving a few blocks took forever and if it rained, or there was an accident, who knew when you'd arrive at your destination. The problem was that no one carpooled in Atlanta and everyone and their mama was "discovering" Atlanta and moving to the area. The HOV lanes were rarely congested. I envied the driver and passengers in those cars and trucks that just whizzed by while the rest of us drove at a snail's pace. I knew they were laughing at us and screaming, "See you later, suckers."

As I briskly walked through the restaurant door, I glanced down at my watch, again. I wasn't too late. Taylor had kept me waiting many times without complaints from me, so today was her turn to wait patiently. It didn't take me long to spot her at the popular after-hours bar. As usual, an attractive gentleman was hanging on her every word. They were seated at the far corner of the bar. Taylor threw her head back and laughed at something he whispered in her ear. She still hadn't spotted me. For good measure, I saw her touch his arm a few times. I swear, girlfriend had the art of flirting down to a science and men just ate it up like a gourmet meal.

I walked the short distance to the bar and noticed I was receiving some admiring glances. I knew from experience not to make eye contact with anyone if I didn't want to be hemmed up by some man with weak conversation trying to get my cell number. Taylor looked up in mid-sentence and spotted me walking her way. She smiled and winked.

"K, there you are. I was wondering what was keeping you," she said, standing, kissing me on the cheek, and offering a warm hug.

"K, this is Walter Roberts. Walter, this is my best friend, Kennedy Logan."

He held out his hand and gave me a firm handshake. "Nice to meet you, Kennedy."

"Same here."

"How did two beautiful women end up best friends?"

"No one else could put up with us," Taylor joked.

They laughed, I didn't. In college, women didn't let Taylor and me get too close to them. They always thought we'd take their men.

"Walter is an attorney at a prestigious law firm in Midtown."

"Great," I stated half-heartedly. Honestly, I couldn't have cared less. At the moment, I didn't care if he was the president of South Africa.

"Actually, he's a partner," Taylor drooled, with her eyes never leaving his. Walter instinctively puffed out his chest just a little further.

"Wonderful."

Walter and I stood there grinning at each other for a few seconds. I glanced at Taylor and gave her that look. The look that screamed, "Dismiss Walter. Like now."

"Well, Walter, you have my business card. Give me a call sometime. Maybe we can hook up for drinks."

"I sure will. Count on it. It was nice meeting you, Kennedy."

"You too, William."

"It's Walter."

"Okay, Walter."

"Take care, ladies, and enjoy the rest of your evening."

Taylor and I excused ourselves and found a table quicker than I expected due to the size of the professional, after-work crowd that had already congregated. Many were still dressed in office attire. Expensive suits and shoes were the uniform of choice. This was truly buppie America at its best.

"K, why you looking so down? I thought you'd be jumping for joy now that you have your apartment back," Taylor asked, sliding herself into our booth.

"Am I that obvious?" I brushed my hair back from my face with both hands.

"Yes, you aren't good at hiding your feelings. You wear them on your sleeve like a badge of honor."

"That's what Drake used to say all the time," I half whispered to myself. "Said anyone could read my face like an open book."

"You mean Drake and I actually agreed on something. Umm, that isn't good. But this mood isn't about Drake. Is it?"

I didn't respond. Just looked out the window as the cars passed by at a snail's pace. I imagined them en route to their families. It appeared everyone had somebody but me.

"K, aren't you over that fool yet? Damn, was the dick that good?"

I instantly looked down and sensed tears forming in my eyes. I blinked rapidly, trying to contain them.

"Kennedy, I'm sorry. I didn't mean to be so harsh, but it has been awhile now. It's time to move on. There are definitely more fish in the sea."

"That's the problem. He won't leave me alone."

"What do you mean?"

"Taylor, at first he was calling me at home. Now, he harasses me at work."

"You're kidding. What kind of harassment?" Taylor questioned with an anxious look on her face.

"He touches me and says disgusting sexual things to me."

"What?"

"Yes. You heard right. I'm not kidding."

"Report him. Report his ass. That's sexual harassment and you don't have to tolerate that. His ass will be fired in a New York minute."

"It's not that simple," I whined.

"Why not? It sounds pretty cut-and-dried to me."

"Well, it's not. It's much more complicated."

"Do you have any witnesses?" she asked.

"No, Drake is pretty good at covering his tracks. He talks a good game and comes across as downright charming. No one would ever think he was capable of the things he has done to me."

"Kennedy, what exactly has he done?"

"Just the other day, he asked to speak with me after a staff meeting. Behind closed doors he started talking about us getting back together and then he had the nerve to fondle my breasts through my blouse."

"Oh, hell no. That dirty dog. And what did you do? I would have slammed him in the balls so fast and hard, he wouldn't have been able to walk straight for the rest of the day. He'd have to crawl back to his office. I guarantee you, he'd think twice about touching me again."

"Well, I'm not you, Taylor."

"What did you do?"

"Nothing. What was I suppose to do? I couldn't cause a scene at work and Drake and I, at one point, did have a relationship."

"Kennedy, sweetie. I don't care. The relationship is over. 'Had' is the key word. Drake had absolutely no right to touch you, to put his hands on you. And now, he probably thinks he can do it again since you didn't set him straight. That arrogant bastard."

I looked over at the bar. The crowd had thinned out some, but the drinks were still flowing heavily.

"I knew there were multiple reasons I can't stand his tired ass. And you mentioned things; what other things has Drake done to you that I'm not aware of?"

Our waitress chose that moment to walk over and take our order. I was no longer hungry. Eating took too much energy out of me. As Taylor rattled off an order of hot wings, side salad, and whatever else she could gulp down without gaining a single ounce, I walked over to the bar to get us two apple martinis. I needed some air and, for once, a good stiff drink.

I placed our drink orders and was patiently waiting for the bartender to return. I glanced around at the crowd and noticed a few couples huddled up together. I imagined they whispered sweet nothings in each others' ears. Why couldn't I meet an attractive, nice, decent man? What made me attract dogs?

"Hi, Miss Logan."

"Hello, uh . . ."

"Michael. Michael Hanson."

"That's right. I never forget a face, but I'm horrible with names. You work in the communications/marketing department, don't you?"

"Yes." He smiled. "And you work in customer service."

Michael's department worked on my floor, on the opposite side. They were a small group of six people: three women and three men. Michael was an average-looking guy who I'd passed in the hallway on occasion, or saw in the company cafeteria, usually eating alone. He wasn't drop-dead gorgeous or anything, but he appeared to have a warm, inviting personality that shined through and made you look twice.

"I haven't seen you around lately."

"Huh?" I asked, coming out of my trance.

"I was just saying, I haven't seen you on the floor lately."

"I was out sick for a while and now I'm keeping a low profile; trying to catch up on my work."

"Oh, I see. That explains it. Well, I've missed your pretty smile."

As if on cue, I looked up and smiled brightly.

"That's the one."

"Thank you." I blushed.

"You're welcome. You always wear such a lovely smile for everyone. Sometimes, when I pass you in the hallway, that smile is just what I need at that moment. It stays with me for the remainder of the day, like a ray of sunshine."

I beamed again. "Now, you have me blushing like a schoolgirl."

"I didn't mean to. I'm only being honest."

"Do you come here often?" I asked.

We laughed at the same time because my comment sounded so cliché.

"No, actually, a coworker is celebrating a birthday. So, my team brought him over here for a quick drink or two."

"That's sweet."

"This is convenient to the office."

"I'm here with my girlfriend." I pointed to Taylor who was looking at me and silently screaming for me to hurry up.

"Listen, since you and Mr. Collins aren't dating anymore, I would love to take you out to dinner sometime. Get to know you and that smile better."

Everything around me slowed down. "What did you say?"

"I'd like to take you out to dinner sometime?" Michael repeated with confusion registering on his face.

"No, the other comment."

"What? Since you and Mr. Collins aren't—"

"Yeah, that part. What would give you the idea that Drake—Mr. Collins—and I were dating?"

Michael shifted uncomfortably from one foot to the other. "You know how people talk. People hear and see things and the gossip mill gets to running. I apologize if I—"

"No, no, it's okay. I can't believe this," I half murmured to myself.

"Are you all right?" Michael asked with concern clearly written on his face.

"Yeah, sure." The bartender had returned with my drinks. I quickly paid him and was about to walk off. My temporary smile had vanished and Michael was forgotten.

"Do you need any help with your drinks? I'd be happy to carry them over to your table."

"No, thank you, Michael. I can handle them."

"Well, don't forget about my offer."

"Huh?"

"My offer to take you out sometime. For dinner and drinks."

"Thanks, but no thanks. I'm not dating right now."

"Too bad."

"And I'm not interested in starting a new relationship right now."

"I understand and have to respect that then."

"Thank you."

"Well, I'll see you around, and I hope you'll change your mind in the near future. I'm not looking for anything deep. I'd just love to get to know you better."

"I don't think so," I said, shaking my head.

"Well, that's my loss."

I made it back to our table without spilling the drinks, and my head was still spinning over the news I'd just heard.

"What was that all about?" Taylor asked, pointing back in Michael's direction.

"Oh, that was a guy who works in communications on my floor. He was just being nice and saying hello."

"He's kinda cute in a geeky sort of way," Taylor explained, glancing back at him.

"Geeky sort of way?"

"Yeah. He's no Drake in the looks department, but he does have a presence about him."

"Quit staring."

"I'm not."

"He knew about me and Drake."

"Knew what?" Taylor asked, sipping on her drink.

"That we had a relationship outside of work."

"You're kidding," Taylor said, stopping in mid-drink.

"No. I wish I were. He said several people on the floor know."

"I'm not surprised. It's hard to keep office romances a secret. People can pick up on that sort of thing. A certain look exchanged. An insignificant touch. People, especially women, can tell when a woman has been intimate with a man. You just get this vibe. I can't explain it. It's in the body language."

"That's all I need," I cried, putting my head in my hands.

"K, I know there is more going on here. It's not the end of the world. So what if they know? I've tried to be patient and wait for you to tell me the entire story in your own time."

"And I will. I'm not ready yet."

"K, I don't judge. You know that. You can tell me anything and that's not going to change my opinion of you. I love you, and my opinion of Drake is already set in stone. You have always been this way with me; afraid I'm going to judge you. So you tell me things on a need-to-know basis."

"I'm just trying to get my act together right now and figure out some things. Try to be patient awhile longer." I managed a stiff smile.

"Talking about a situation can work wonders. Verbalizing it puts situations into perspective."

"Soon, I promise."

"How is your search coming? You haven't updated me in a few days."

"Not much has changed from the last time we talked. I provided what little information I knew and faxed the documents Mother had. Now, I'm playing a waiting game."

"Don't worry, it'll work out like it should. I'm still so honored you confided in me about your desire to find her."

"I am glad too. You've been such a great support system."

"Now, hand me your plate. I ordered thirty hot wings, extra crispy, extra hot. Dig in. I can't eat all these by myself."

I laughed and shook my head.

"What?" Taylor asked with sauce on her fingers, looking up with no clue.

"Nothing. Nothing at all." I smiled. I was happy to have Taylor as a friend. She made my day and didn't even realize it.

"What do you think of Walter over there?" At that exact moment, Walter looked over and waved at us.

"I only talked to him for a few minutes. He's all right."

"He has a cabin on Lake Lanier."

"Cool."

"And, he's only thirty-two and already a partner at his law firm."

"Impressive."

"Is that all you can say?"

"Taylor, what do you want me to say?"

"I don't know, but something other than *impressive*."

"When are you two going out because I know you will?"

"I predict I'll be hearing from Mr. Roberts by the end of the week."

"I'm sure you will."

We both giggled. I believed money and power were better than sex to Taylor.

"Oh, I forgot to tell you. Guess who Mother talked to the other night?" I asked, licking sauce from my fingers.

"Who?"

"Guess?"

"I don't feel like guessing, just tell me."

I gave Taylor a look.

"No. I know you're kidding? Mrs. Logan talked to her ex? Your daddy?"

"Yep."

"Oh, what I would have given to be a fly on her wall."

"She said they talked for about two hours."

"Talked or screamed at one another?"

"Mother said it was a liberating and very calm conversation."

"That's deep."

"Tell me about it. I'm glad they finally talked and put some closure to their situation."

"I know what you mean. Years ago, I thought your mom was going to have a nervous breakdown over your daddy."

"She almost did."

"And then she just snapped out of it."

"She said she prayed about it."

I was silently thinking that some men could put you through some serious changes all in the name of love.

"I never understood what your dad was thinking. Dumping your mom for a woman twenty years younger. I never saw that coming. Not in a million years. They always seemed so happy together."

"Neither did Mother."

"Men do that shit all the time, though. They get sick of the old model who was there for them from the very beginning when they didn't have a pot to piss in, but once they get older and successful and the money is rolling in, well, it's time to switch to a newer, younger, and improved model."

Eagerly, I shook my head in agreement.

"But if an older woman goes after a younger man, she's seen as a cougar."

"Double standards."

"Sad, but true. Mrs. Logan should have found herself a nice young stud and got her groove on."

"Taylor."

"What's wrong with that? Why couldn't she enjoy herself too? After thirty years of the same old stuff, I'm sure she wanted some variety. Some young stuff."

"You are too much," I teased.

"My Kennedy."

"My Taylor. Can I tell you something?"

"Of course."

"To be honest, I'm not sure if I want to meet my birth mom if they do find her."

"Why not? Regardless of what she did, you're still a part of her. That's not going to change."

"If I had a child, I could never give up my baby."

"We couldn't, but playing devil's advocate, you don't know what the lady was going through at that time."

"It doesn't matter. I would have made a way."

"Your biological mom did you a favor. You grew up with a wonderful family who loves you like their last breath depends on it."

"You're right, and I count my blessings every day."

"Look at me, you know my history. I have a mother who is working on her fourth marriage and that one isn't going so well. I have had so many stepfathers that I can't even keep track, and my mother equates gifts with love. I would have given anything to have her attend my plays and recitals. Instead, she sent flowers while she was off traveling around the world and

spending one of my stepfather's money," Taylor stated
with a tremble in her voice. I knew this had caused her
much hurt and pain over the years.

"I realize I'm very lucky." I bit into another wing.

"If for nothing else, you deserve answers and inner
peace. Besides, you need to know your medical history."

"I guess."

"Trust me, K. Here, take some more of these wings
while I get us another round of drinks. That bartender
is hooking these up," she stated, rising from the table.

"I don't want any more wings."

"K, take them and quit being difficult. And it's going
to be all right. No matter what is bothering you, it can
only get better." Taylor winked before walking off to
the bar.

On the walk back to our cars, arms linked, we talked
more about Drake.

"Seriously, what are you going to do about him?"

"I haven't figured it out yet."

"Kennedy, I've known you for a long time. Whether
you believe it or not, you are a strong woman. She's
there, inside you, waiting for you to release her. Mr.
and Mrs. Logan have doted on you your entire life, but
you're a grown woman now and you have to handle
your business. Don't be a doormat for that fool."

"I know all this."

"Well, act like you know it. I'm serious, K. Drake
changed you somehow."

"How?" I asked, stopping in mid-stride.

"You stopped thinking for yourself. That's not you.
Drake thrives on control and power; don't give him
yours."

"It may be too late."

"It's never too late. You're a beautiful woman, inside and out, and you deserve someone who's going to treat you special and kind. And with respect. Drake just wanted a beautiful woman on his arm and in his bed. He couldn't care less about your dreams, goals, and aspirations."

"Taylor, I loved him. I really did."

"K, love doesn't hurt and make you lose yourself. Think about it. Drake should love the person you already are, not try to change you into his ideal mate. That Michael guy back in there, I saw how he kept looking at you. Give him a chance."

"I'm definitely not ready to jump back into another relationship."

"I'm not saying right this instant, but give brothers like him a chance. He appeared decent."

"Look who's talking. The lady who uses money and power as a prerequisite."

"I'm talking about you, not me." We both laughed again as we made our way to our cars.

"Whatever."

"Listen, drive carefully and I'll talk to you later in the week," Taylor stated, unlocking her car door and giving me another hug.

"Love ya."

"Love ya back, girl."

Chapter 21

It was a little short of a week later, after our first impromptu business meeting, that I found myself riding the elevator back upstairs for yet another one. My manager had asked me to finish it up, since I started the process, and to report back to her. She claimed that this would be good experience for me. The previous day, I had turned in my findings in a detailed, comprehensive ten-page report. Today was to be a follow-up meeting for all concerned and to tie up loose ends.

As before, I arrived early. Again, I wasn't sure what to expect from Drake after the fiasco from last time. I realized I wouldn't and couldn't allow myself to be alone with him. I had thought long and hard about what Taylor had said, about filing sexual harassment charges, but I wasn't sure. I had no doubt Drake would drag our so-called secret affair into the spotlight and I definitely wasn't ready for that. Drake's family had money, so losing his job wouldn't faze him.

I was totally confused. I had no clue what I should do or how I should proceed. I knew my life was in shambles and I had to do something to move forward and reclaim it.

This time when I arrived on the floor, the conference room wasn't empty. Apparently, another meeting was going on, which was expected to end shortly. I stood outside the door and chatted with the administrative assistant. She was an older black woman, with salt-and-pepper hair, who, I'd heard, had started out as a temp and eventually moved into a permanent position.

"How are you today, Miss Logan?"

"I'm okay and yourself?" I asked.

"I can't complain. I'm here, I'm alive, and I'm kicking. That's a blessing in itself, wouldn't you say?"

I laughed. That sounded like something Mother would say. "It's true."

"Sometimes you young people forget to count your blessings." She winked.

"You might be right."

"I know I am. I have a daughter about your age."

I smiled and looked toward the conference room door. I didn't want a lecture on religion or the state of the younger generation.

"If I may say so, you're smart, gorgeous, and seem like a wonderful person who was brought up right."

"Thank you."

"I mean it. Your mother should be very proud of you. I noticed you months ago. You stand out around here because of the way you carry yourself with such grace. You don't gossip and be all up into everyone's business. You have class."

"Thank you, that's very sweet," I stated, again glancing back at the conference room.

I noticed the other meeting was ending, as associates walked out of the conference room, scattering in different directions. I saw a few familiar faces and I waved.

"I like conversing with young people, and I think they like talking to me because I call it as I see it. I'm real, as you say. For you, I have one simple piece of advice:

remember, what looks good isn't always pretty," she said, raising her eyebrows.

I opened my mouth to ask her what she meant by that, but Drake and a very lovely woman with legs from here to eternity and a Halle Berry short hairstyle came around the corner and I didn't get the opportunity. I'd never seen the woman on the floor before.

"Excuse me," the mystery woman stated in a condescending tone as she stuck her nose up at me and briskly walked around me.

I moved out of the way. Drake barely acknowledged me.

"Miss Logan, the meeting is starting in just a few minutes," he stated, looking down at his watch as if I was running late.

I delivered a half smile to the administrative assistant. "I guess that's my clue to go."

"Sure, darling. You take care of yourself," she replied.

"By the way, who was the woman with Mr. Collins?" I asked.

"Oh, that's Miss Reynolds. She started a week ago. Replacing the management slot that was vacated by Mr. Stephenson."

"Umm. I see."

By the time I made it into the conference room, I had to sit closer to the front and to Drake. I noticed every now and then Miss Reynolds glaring at me out of the corner of my eye. I couldn't figure out for the life of me why I was getting strong vibes that she didn't care for me. This from a woman I hadn't even had the opportunity to be formally introduced to, or knew existed until a few moments ago.

"Good morning, everyone. Today's meeting should

be short and sweet," Drake announced, his eyes lingering on me for a few additional seconds. Miss Reynolds caught him and openly frowned at me.

"Before we go any further, for those of you who haven't had the opportunity to meet her yet, I'd like to introduce you to Miss Brittany Reynolds. She's one of our new managers."

She waved and stood briefly. "Thank you, Mr. Collins. I look forward to meeting everyone and fostering productive and meaningful working relationships. I'll be making my way around to meet with some of you in the next few days."

"Okay, let's get down to business. The first item on the agenda is . . ."

The meeting went by quickly, and the good news was that we were able to pacify our clients with some modifications on how we handle their accounts. Bottom line, they were no longer pulling out, and our working relationship would continue.

Throughout the meeting, I noticed a silent communication going on between Drake and Miss Reynolds. It was very subtle, but there nevertheless. I knew it wasn't my imagination because it was how we used to act with each other in public. I immediately picked up on the vibes they were giving off to one another.

Finally, the meeting ended and I couldn't wait to get off that floor. I retrieved my legal pad, purse, and pen, and was trying to slip quietly away. Of course, that wasn't in Drake's plan.

"Miss Logan, have you been formally introduced to Miss Reynolds?" he inquired. He was trying to be funny and I hated him for it. I knew what was going on; he was messing with me.

I turned around with a smile plastered on my face. Drake and Brittany were standing side by side, looking at me expectantly. "No, I haven't." I reached out my hand. "Good to meet you. I'm Kennedy Logan."

"Brittany Reynolds. Kennedy, what a lovely name."

"Thank you."

"You're one of those relations service reps, aren't you?"

"Yes, I'm one of those." I immediately didn't like her condescending tone.

"I must come down there and check out the team. I haven't been in the trenches in a while." Then she laughed a shrill, irritating cackle.

"You do that."

"I told Brittany what a wonderful team you and I made behind closed doors, working on our project," Drake injected, emphasizing "working."

"Did you?" I said, knowing what he was insinuating.

"Drake and I have spent an enormous amount of time behind closed doors as well," Brittany said. "So, your services won't be needed anytime soon."

"Good for him."

"Drake is showing me the ropes, so to speak." She laughed, daring me to read between the lines.

Heifer, I silently screamed. "Well, it was nice meeting you. Take care."

"You too, Kendall."

"That's Kennedy."

"Oh, I'm sorry. Of course, Kennedy."

I bet you are. Heifer.

With them not too far behind me, I started to make my exit and escape. I could hear them whispering and laughing behind my back and having too much fun.

Yes, they were very comfortable with each other. As much as I despised Drake, I still felt a twinge of jealousy.

"Miss Logan, may I speak to you for a moment?"

With a scowl on my face, I walked over to the administrative assistant's desk.

"Yes?" I asked, slightly annoyed. I just wanted to get back to my floor, to the security of my cubicle, and hide out for the remainder of the day.

"I know this is none of my business, but as I said before, you seem like a nice girl. You remind me of my own daughter with your mild demeanor. Since I consider myself a Christian lady, I figure it is my duty to speak with you. God don't like ugly."

I was getting sick to my stomach as I watched Drake and Miss Reynolds walk conspiratorially down the hallway together. I couldn't pull my eyes off them. An image of the two of them embraced in the heat of passion flashed before my eyes.

"Watch your back with him."

"Him. Him who?"

"Mr. Collins."

"Mr. Collins? I don't understand." She had my attention now.

"I don't want to get all up in your business, but I hear things. Management tends to forget we are in the room."

"Things like what? You hear what?" I asked, getting a sinking feeling in the pit of my stomach.

"Unfortunately, not good."

"Please tell me if they concern me."

"Well, I don't want to cause any trouble and lose my job. I have bills . . ."

"You won't. This is between you and I. This won't go any further; you have my word."

"I've overheard Mr. Collins discussing your personal relationship with Mr. Brewster."

"Mr. Brewster?"

"Mr. Collins was bragging about how you were not as hard to get next to as he had been led to believe. Supposedly, he had been told you were a challenge when he moved here from LA and he set out to prove Mr. Brewster wrong."

"What?"

"There was other stuff said and, believe me, it isn't fit to repeat. I think what happens between a man and a woman should remain between—"

I cut her off and started to walk away. "Thank you, I appreciate your information."

"Baby, you need to check that Drake Collins and put him in his proper place," she whispered.

Mr. Brewster was one of the oldest black managers on the floor. He was a senior vice president with the longest tenure. Why in the world was Drake discussing our relationship with him, or anyone for that matter? I was totally speechless.

Chapter 22

A couple of weeks later I got up the nerve to call Drake and invite him to lunch. It was finally time for us to talk. Luckily, I was able to leave the invite on his voice mail. I didn't know if it was me, or if I was just being self-conscious. It seemed more and more people were whispering and staring when I walked on the floor. I had to put a stop to Drake's spreading of vicious rumors and to let him know that there was no possibility of us getting back together. Ever. His actions had made sure of that.

I asked him to meet me at Gorin's, around the corner from our building. I figured as long as we were in a public setting, it wouldn't be a big deal that we were eating lunch together. For all anyone knew, we could have been having a business lunch and discussing a client. And even better, Drake couldn't try anything with an audience. Around one o'clock, I made the short walk over. I had serious butterflies in my stomach. I was extremely nervous about seeing him again and talking. Sometimes Drake intimidated me and had a way of twisting things around to make me appear stupid. I was determined not to let that happen this time.

When I walked through the doors, initially I didn't see Drake seated at the back booth. Then I heard his deep voice. He was in conversation with one of the ladies from my floor. Connie was flirting her butt off and making sure her more than ample cleavage was smack in his face. I knew Drake was drooling because he loved big breasts. At one point, he had tried to talk me into getting breast implants because he said they would make me sexier. He was even willing to pay for the procedure.

I ignored them and walked over to the counter to place my usual order. By the time I had my almond chicken sandwich, chips, pickle, and soda, Connie had headed out the door and back to work, with Drake now checking out her ample rear end.

I strolled over and slowly seated myself at Drake's booth. The restaurant wasn't that crowded. Only a few other customers were quietly eating, or reading the newspaper or a book. The bulk of the rush-hour lunch crowd had dissipated. Ironically, Drake had ordered the same meal I had except for the soda.

"Hello. You look pretty today," he stated, brushing my hair out of my face. I tensed from his touch.

"Hey. We need to talk," I blurted out right away.

"You still don't have any manners? You can't say thank you when someone gives you a compliment?" he asked, offended.

"I didn't come here for compliments. We need to talk."

"Talk then," he shouted.

"Why are you spreading nasty rumors about me?"

"I don't know what you're talking about."

"Like hell."

"Kennedy, cursing doesn't become you."

"Drake, why are you doing this to me?"

"I've already told you, I don't know what you're talking about.

"I don't believe you."

"Are you calling me a liar?"

"If the shoe fits."

"You're pretty bold sitting up in this restaurant talking all this smack. If we were behind closed doors, you wouldn't be so bad."

"I repeat, why are you doing this to me? Because I broke up with you?"

"Correction, I broke it off with your ass. Don't get it twisted. I can't have a girlfriend who I can't trust further than I can throw her."

"Is that really the way you've placed what happened in that twisted, sick mind of yours?"

"I didn't agree to meet you to listen to your insults, baby."

"The truth hurts, doesn't it?"

"Yeah, I guess it does since you can't seem to admit to any of yours," he accused.

"You really believe your lies, don't you?"

Drake clapped his hands three times. "You know, I applaud you, Kennedy. For once, you are standing up for yourself."

"I got sick and tired of people like you using and abusing me."

"I didn't do anything to you that you didn't enjoy."

"I thought we could discuss this like two mature adults. I see I was wrong as usual when it concerns you. There is only one adult here today and it's not you."

I still hadn't touched my sandwich. Only taken a few sips of soda.

Glancing at my soda, he said, "I thought you had stopped drinking sodas. How many times do I have to tell you those things are not good for you? Drink water."

"No, *you* wanted me to stop. And you still haven't answered my question." I took another long sip as Drake leaned back, giving me his full attention.

"What question?"

"Drake, please, playing stupid doesn't become you. Let me go. I'm not the one for you. I never was."

"Kennedy, I don't know what illusions you have in that pretty little head of yours, but I'm not restraining you. I've moved on."

"With Miss Reynolds?"

"And if I have, what's it to you?"

I shook my head. "It doesn't even matter."

"Oh, it matters. You can't stand the thought of me inside her."

"You're sick, you know that? You derive pleasure out of degrading others. Does that make you feel bigger? More of a man?"

"No, the problem is that you couldn't please your man and then to do what you did."

I felt tears forming in my eyes. "Will you just shut up talking about that night? Shut up. That wasn't my fault."

"Oh, here come the tears. Why wasn't it your fault? You let it happen. And I thought I could trust you," he whispered, leaning in closer to me.

With tears in my eyes, I leaned back in the booth. "I can't believe I thought I loved you at one time; I would have done anything for you. I let you take me places no other man had ever taken me." I sighed. "God, I was so wrong. You are so handsome on the outside, but inside you are ugly and evil."

Drake reached up to caress my cheek. "I never forced you to do anything you didn't want to do. In fact, I never laid a hand on you. Never hit you or raised my voice to you in aggression. Remember that."

"That's what's so sad. I fell willingly into your trap."

Suddenly, Drake's demeanor changed. "Baby, I know you don't believe me, but I do love you. And I miss you. Brittany doesn't mean a damn thing to me. She's just something to do to pass the time."

"Love me? Huh? You don't know the meaning of the word. You only love yourself and that big, massive ego of yours. You wouldn't know how to begin to give love, only how to possess."

"Let's give it another try. I'll make it up to you, Kennedy. I promise. We can go away for the weekend and talk some more."

"You haven't heard a word I said. It's over. Leave me alone."

"Let's go check into the hotel across the street," he said, reaching for my hand. "I'll make you feel so good."

"Let go of me. I knew this would be a waste of time," I said, rising to leave. "You haven't heard a word I have said. I need to learn to trust my better judgment. This was a mistake."

"Where are you going?"

"Anywhere but here. Call one of your other women."

He leaned in closer. "But, I wanna eat *your* pussy. I miss that little moan you make right before you come in my mouth."

"I hate your ass," I screamed, throwing my cup of soda in his lap.

"You crazy bitch. This isn't over. Not by a long shot," he screamed, jumping up and grabbing paper napkins off the table.

"Oh, yes, it is. If you bother me again, I promise I'll file sexual harassment charges against you."

"And who do you think they'll believe? I'll air all your filthy laundry. We both know it's pretty dirty."

"I did all those things to please you."

"You'll be the one who comes across looking like a slut."

I shook my head in disbelief. "Just stay away from me, or better yet, drop dead," I screamed, running out the door.

After that disastrous lunch encounter, I went to extreme measures to avoid seeing Drake. I came to the conclusion that he wasn't one to be rational with. According to the rumor mill circulating throughout the office, he and Brittany were hitting it hard and strong. *Better her than me. Let him stick his dirty dick in her.* Maybe he'd forget about me and concentrate on making somebody else's life miserable.

Drake and Brittany deserved each other. Her reputation as a backbiting, backstabbing, and conniving female was quickly spreading. Most associates agreed that the "b" in her first name stood for something other than Brittany.

Chapter 23

I was minding my own business the following Thursday. I had returned from walking down to the Varsity restaurant for onion rings and a vanilla milk shake. I wasn't really looking at my surroundings, or paying much attention to anyone or anything in particular.

I was in my own little world. The night before, Mother told me that she and Daddy had talked again, for almost another two hours. I could hear the excitement and happiness as it seeped into her voice. I was happy for them. I smiled warmly inside because I knew she had never stopped loving Daddy and she had finally forgiven him. One day I hoped to find true love. Someone who complemented me as opposed to diminishing my spirit. In the meantime, I was willing to be by myself and love myself.

I had walked into the building, approaching the security desk, when I spotted *them* coming in my direction. I panicked. I was like a deer caught in blaring headlights. Totally blind. For a few brief seconds, I stood there with a shocked expression on my face and my mouth wide open. I wanted to run and hide. I frantically looked from side to side, but there was nowhere to escape. I noticed a few people pass by and look at me curiously as my heartbeat sped up. I couldn't catch my breath; I thought I would hyperventilate on the spot.

My palms were sweaty. I dropped my bag of onion rings and stooped to retrieve them with my head spinning the entire time.

By this time, Drake and his brother had spotted me and were headed my way. Drake was dressed casually in khaki pants and a polo shirt. As usual, he was looking like he stepped off the pages of *GQ* magazine. I looked away and my mind went blank. All I could think about was how my vanilla milk shake was melting and how my onion rings were getting cold.

"Blake, you remember Kennedy, don't you?" Drake asked, standing directly in front of me. Only a few inches separated us.

"Of course, how could I forget this lovely lady?" he stated, pulling me close for a hug.

"Blake is in town for a couple of days."

I still hadn't uttered a single word.

"Can you believe I was able to convince my brother to cut his day short and put in a few rounds of golf?" Blake asked.

I looked from one to the other.

"Do you play?" Blake inquired.

"Kennedy?" Drake laughed, answering for me. "Kennedy's sport is just looking pretty."

"It's a damn shame that you and Drake split up. I thought you were good for him. You slowed my brother down and tamed his wild ass."

"I've got to go," I barely whispered.

"Now, he's going to revert to his old shenanigans. Running the streets."

Drake wasn't saying much, just standing there with this amused look on his face.

"I'm late, I've got to get back to work."

"Oh, we're sorry. Didn't mean to keep you," Blake insisted.

"No, we wouldn't think of getting you in trouble with your manager," Drake stated.

"Well, Kennedy. Maybe Drake and I can take you out to dinner one night before I leave. I'd love to see you again. Relive old times."

I didn't answer. "I gotta go," I stated, walking away, almost running.

"Okay. See you around."

"Real soon," Drake interjected.

I managed to make it to the elevator, ride up to my floor, and head straight to the restroom. And then, I broke down. I was a mess. I threw up two times with my head stuck in the commode. I started crying and couldn't stop. My nose was running. Ten minutes later I was walking back out the door, on my way home. I couldn't even remember what I murmured to my manager. I knew I had to get out of there. Away from Drake and Blake.

I managed to drive home, and went straight to bed. Sleep was my escape. My salvation from my inner demons.

Chapter 24

When I would hear stories of people committing suic-ide, I used to wonder what could drive a person to such an extreme, selfish act. I would think they were such cowards. Too afraid, or spineless, or weak to address and deal with whatever was beating them down. They would simply give up and take the easy way out. I could never come up with any example, reason, or circumstance as to why I would end my life. Life is too precious. You only get one chance, this isn't a dress rehearsal. There is no coming back. Now, I know differently.

I've heard people say, "God doesn't give us more than we can bear." Well, sometimes He does. Sometimes life becomes too overwhelming. Sometimes events occur that are too difficult to face on a day-to-day, ongoing basis. It's just easier to end it all than live the event over and over and over. It's so much easier not trying to wear the happy face when the heart and spirit are broken beyond repair.

I used to wonder why, during slavery days, we never heard tales of slaves killing themselves in mass suicides. What did they have to live for: to never see their countries again, to be separated from their spouse and children, to be raped and violated, to be treated like a piece of property when some of them were descendants

of kings and queens. What did they have to live for?
Then I realized that through all the trials and tribulations, they still had one thing. Hope. Hope that one day
they'd see their homelands. Hope that their offspring
would live better lives. Hope that they'd one day be
free.

I didn't have any more hope. That had all been
crushed in one deceitful act. I had nothing but despair,
and despair was nothing. After seeing Drake and Blake
yesterday, it all came rushing back at me like a big slap
in the face. Like a train head-on. And the two of them
stood there, grinning like nothing was wrong. Pretending. It was all a horrible illusion. Now, I remembered
everything. Every disgusting detail.

What makes one want to end it all? Let me tell you.
These are my true confessions.

Dear Journal,

*As I said before, Drake was the man I wanted
to marry and have beautiful children with. I
knew he wasn't perfect, but neither was I. Taylor
and Mother didn't understand our relationship.
They hadn't been there through our ups and
downs, our trials and tribulations. They weren't
there to see the side of Drake who let me cry on
his shoulder and held me close as I agonized over
finding my birth mom. They didn't see the man
who ran me hot bubble baths and gently brushed
my hair like I was a precious baby.*

*I was even able to talk myself into accepting
some of his unconventional sexual quirks. Drake
was a man and men had strong sexual appe-
tites. Some stronger than others. I understood
that Drake bored easily and he had to maintain*

excitement in his life. That's why he loved hunting and hiking and golfing and football. It was all about the thrill of the game. So, yes, I would maintain excitement for my man and be sexy and open-minded.

After each breakup, I really psyched myself up in order to rationalize him being back in my life. And, of course, Drake came back with every desire to please me. He knew the right words to speak, the correct gifts to buy, and the right places to take me. All to make me fall swiftly back under his spell. That didn't last long. When all was said and done, it was always about Drake. Always Drake. Whatever lies and misdeeds he had to tell and do to achieve his happiness, he did it. The truth was boring and his motives were always the ultimate goal.

Last year, it was a few days after Christmas and Drake and I had spent an enormous amount of time together. I had taken some of my vacation days and so had he. So we were inseparable. He had pretty much moved into my place. Drake had clothes in my closet, his toothbrush and shaving kit in my bathroom. I helped him Christmas shop for his mom and dad, we checked out The Nutcracker at the Fox Theater, and enjoyed the holidays together doing other festive things like attending The Festival of Trees. The Christmas season had always been my favorite time of the year. During this time, I reverted to being a little girl. I was on cloud nine and all was good in my world.

It was a few days before New Year's Day, a

Friday night, and Drake and I had attended a post-Christmas party with some of his friends. I swear, the man had been in Atlanta only briefly, yet he had more friends than I did, and I had lived here all my life. People were naturally drawn to him.

Drake and I had a great time. It was a small, intimate affair. There were about six couples total and we sat around and sipped wine, ate delicious food, played board games, and talked. A real low-key event; just my speed. Drake was very relaxed and especially attentive to my needs.

I drank a bit too much, which was anything over two glasses, but I'd noticed that whenever I was with Drake he encouraged me to let loose. I knew if I was with him, he'd take care of me and not let anything horrible happen.

I truly enjoyed myself and no one could have told me that that would be the last time Drake and I was together as a couple. We laughed, we cuddled, and we kissed under the mistletoe. It was a magical evening, and there were even a few snow flurries in the crisp air that added to the magical spell. We left the party around midnight and I convinced him to drive around to look at Christmas lights and decorations before they were taken down.

Drake and I drove around, listened to Christmas music on the radio, laughed, and had a great time in the sanctity of his car. It was like it was just he and I in our own little world. We sipped on some hot cider, taken from the party, that was laced with liquor, and I was feeling no pain.

I was buzzed, but I didn't care. I felt free and in love. I knew Drake had his imperfections, but I knew he'd change for me. Love could do that . . . change a person. It was almost a new year, with new beginnings.

We arrived back at my apartment a little after one A.M. The apartment was nice and cozy. Without turning on the lights in the living room, I asked Drake to turn on the Christmas lights on my tree while I took a hot shower. I wanted to slip into something sexy, this Frederick's of Hollywood outfit I'd purchased complete with Santa boots. It was Drake's last present that he had to open. Ho. Ho. Ho.

After I couldn't convince Drake to join me in the shower, I slipped in alone. I turned the water to as hot as I could stand it, placed my face under the showerhead, and enjoyed the feel of the hot water streaming down my face. I relived our night together and smiled because it wasn't over yet.

I vaguely heard Drake rambling around in the bedroom and kitchen. He had said that he was going to get the rest of the champagne out of the fridge. We had a leftover bottle from a few days earlier that he'd spent an enormous amount of money on. I stepped out of the shower, layered myself with body lotion and spritz, and slipped on my sexy lingerie. I pinned my hair up on top of my head, pulled on my black and red Santa boot slippers, and walked back into my bedroom.

Drake was already under the covers, completely nude and waiting for me. He reached out his hand, pulled back the covers, and I slipped under after tossing my boots to the floor.

"You are so beautiful. You know that," Drake stated, propped up on his elbows, caressing my cheek.

"You are too."

He gave me a funny look. "What? Men can't be beau-tiful."

"Well, you are, babe."

"I think you have definitely had too much to drink," he declared.

"You think so?"

"Yes, definitely," he said, pulling down my red spaghetti strap and pouring some chilled champagne, from the nightstand, on my nipples.

He proceeded to lick it off, and I proceeded to melt.

"Oh, you like that, huh, Miss Claus?" he asked, searching between my legs to see if I was ready.

I nodded.

"Well, Santa has more where that came from."

"Oh really?"

"Have you been a naughty girl? Or a good girl?"

"Good."

"Come here. We'll have to correct that." Drake flipped me over onto my stomach and discarded my gown. So much for the $125 I spent. He poured champagne in the arch of my back and proceeded to lick and suck it off, all the way down to my buttocks. That night, it was all about me. Drake pleased me from the tip of my toes to the top of my head and I got to ride his reindeer. Afterward, we lay *wrapped in each other's arms with our legs entwined. I let out a pleased, satisfied sigh.*

"I could get used to this, babe."

Drake had his eyes closed and his arms wrapped protectively around me.

Silence.

"Did you hear what I said?"

"Shhh. Just relax. Go to sleep," he murmured in a drowsy voice.

Cradled in the arms of the man I loved, I did just that. I dozed off into a peaceful, dream-filled sleep while visions of family, children, and marriage danced through my head. In my sleep-induced state, I vaguely remember Drake getting up to go to the restroom. He was soon back, claiming his rightful spot. Nestled next to me. I quickly dozed back off.

I don't know how much time passed; I was disoriented and shrouded in the throes of deep sleep. I felt Drake gently nudging me and kissing my neck. His hardness pressed against me.

"Babe, go back to sleep," I whispered, reaching behind me to stroke his cheek.

Drake didn't say anything. He continued to spoon with me and caress my breasts. As usual, he knew my nipples were one of my weak spots. He started playing with them, squeezing them between his thumb and finger, and I started moaning. Sleep was quickly slipping away. We were still naked from earlier, and I felt the heat rise from his body. I reached back to stroke his erection.

"Oh, I thought you'd like that. I see Rudolph the

red-nosed reindeer is awake to drive his sleigh,"
I teased.

I still had my eyes closed as I continued to
stroke him up and down. Fast and slow. Just like
he liked. At some point, Drake reached around
and inserted three of his fingers inside me. I was
already wet and very excited. I turned around
on my back and spread my legs wider so that he
could continue to do what he was doing so well.
My hand pressed down on his to encourage him
not to stop.

I wanted him then. He could forget foreplay.
I needed to feel him inside me, again. Drake had
other ideas because when I tried to mount him,
he stopped me and pulled my head down near his
lap. Through the darkness of the room, he looked
at me and smiled. I knew what he wanted. I went
to work with a passion. I licked, sucked, squeezed,
and sucked some more. Taking it all in. I'd glance
up and see him trying to hold his moans in.

"That's enough for you, you greedy boy," I
joked, coming up for air. "It's time for you to eat
your supper," I teased.

Through the eerie shadows of my room, Drake
looked at me with this strange glow in his eyes.

"Come on, babe, go down on me. You know I
love that."

Drake went to work; it was his best performance
ever. The man had a true talent for going
downtown. When I was on the verge of coming, I
pushed him off me. I wanted to feel that delicious
dick inside me before I came.

Drake was more than ready to oblige. He eased

me onto all fours and slowly eased himself inside me. I was taken aback for a moment because he felt larger or wider or something that I couldn't quite put my finger on. His thrusts felt like they were coming out my stomach. They had never felt that way before, and he smelled different, too. I assumed it was the new cologne he had recently purchased.

"Oh, babe. You feel so good."

Drake didn't say anything. He continued to ram me with no mercy. His fingers were clawing at my breasts.

"Babe, slow down. There's more where this came from. Quit being so greedy."

I looked back, and Drake had his attention focused on the task at hand. By now, he was usually saying all kinds of nasty shit to me. He loved to talk dirty to me during sex. Instead of turning me off, I'd get super hot. I was pretty verbal myself now and initially that surprised me, but Drake preferred it that way. That early morning, he was uncharacteristically quiet. Too silent. All I heard from him was his heavy panting.

"Oh, babe, your dick is making my pussy feel so good. You've got me so hot."

He was still ramming me with no sign of slowing down.

"That's right. Take what's yours. Oh, God. You've got me cumming. I'm cumming, babe."

We both came at the same time in hard, forceful, spastic shudders. I felt him shoot hot squirts up inside me. At the exact moment that was happening, I heard a cell phone go off in my closet.

Without an ounce of energy left, I collapsed down on the bed. At first, I thought I was imagining things. I dismissed the sound. But then I heard movement.

"What? What is that? Did you hear that?" I asked, crouching on my bed, ready to flee.

Sprawled out on the bed, Drake looked at me in surprise and stared at the closed closet door. Then the door swung wide open and there stood Drake. I looked from one to the other in amazement. There were two Drakes.

"What the hell?" I asked, jumping up and trying to hide my nakedness.

Then Drake spoke. From the closet entrance. "Calm down, Kennedy."

"What do you mean calm down?" I asked, glancing from him to the Drake on the bed, whose dick was now erect and pointing wickedly at me. "Drake, what's going on?" By now, I was crying as the realization of what had happened was slowly sinking in.

The Drake from the closet closed the gap between us.

"That's my identical twin brother, Blake," he said, pointing to the man now hurriedly pulling on his pants.

"What? Your twin. You let your goddamn twin brother fuck me? You bastard. I can't believe this. My God, you're sick," I screamed.

"Calm down, Kennedy," Drake was saying, walking toward me with outstretched hands.

"Don't you touch me. Don't you ever touch me again."

As he tried to calm me, Drake and I wrestled around on my bed.

"Take your hands off me. Both of you get out of my house."

"Man, you'd better calm your hysterical girlfriend down," Blake stated off to the side.

"I thought you loved me. But you had the audacity to let your brother sex me while you watched in the closet like a damn pervert."

"Kennedy, listen to me," Drake screamed, grabbing my shoulder.

"Let me go. That motherfucker raped me. I'm calling the police."

I was still attempting to get out of Drake's arms. He had my arms pinned in front of me, sitting in his lap with my back to his stomach, with both his arms at my side. I struggled. Blake appeared bored with the entire situation.

I managed to free myself when he momentarily loosened his grip, thinking I had calmed down. I tried turning and kicking him in the groin and he slapped me, hard. I screamed and lunged for the phone on the nightstand. Blake casually ripped the cord from the wall and threw the phone out of my reach.

"Listen, man, I'm not going to jail over some pussy, no matter how good it was," Blake declared.

"Shut up, both of you," Drake shouted out of frustration. Rubbing his face between his hands, he screamed, "Let me think."

"You said she'd never know the difference. Why didn't you turn off your damn phone?"

"I'm going to report this. You are not getting

away with this." I tried to run into the living room to retrieve my cell phone from my purse.

Drake threw me back down on the bed, on my back. "What are you going to report?" he questioned with fury in his eyes.

Now, I was afraid and shivering and trying to cover myself with the bed sheet.

"You planned this and you let him rape me," I whispered. "You even watched."

"Raped you? You were enjoying it, tremendously, from what I could see in the closet. You were all over my brother's dick."

"I thought it was you. I thought I was making love to you," I screamed.

"Yeah, right. Blake was tearing up your stuff. You know my shit ain't nine inches long."

I started crying. Drake was furious and Blake was disinterested.

"Call the police and I'll explain how we play these games. How you wanted to get it on with two brothers. We talked about bringing another person into our bed. You try reporting this and I'll make your shit look so stank."

"Why? I loved you," I questioned as I stood and slinked to the floor in a huddle, covering my nakedness the best I could with my hands.

Drake looked at me with disgust. "You never loved me. You couldn't even tell that wasn't me touching you. You don't even know me."

"You're right. I don't know you. You're sick—"

"How you gonna let my brother bang you without knowing the difference? You were sucking his dick. You supposed to be my woman. You should know how I touch you and make you feel."

Blake was still standing off to the side like he was bored silly. I was lying on the floor with my head on the bed and Drake was towering over me. Screaming down at me.

"Drake, man, give her some clothes," Blake said with an ounce of sympathy.

Drake tossed me my gown and I quickly pulled it over my head. My cries were mere moans as I rocked back and forth on the floor with snot running down near my lips.

Drake walked back over and cuddled my head in his hand. "Kennedy, you need to think about this rape allegation. You don't want to make yourself look bad. We had some fun tonight. No one was hurt. Let's leave it at that." He continued to massage my scalp.

"You tricked me. I didn't even know you had a twin brother. I just knew you had a brother in LA."

"Kennedy, nobody tricked you. At some point, you had to realize that wasn't me and you were still into it. You got off. Admit it."

"Just go," I whispered,

"What are you going to do?"

I continued to rock back and forth. It didn't even matter that my nakedness was still showing through my gown for Drake and Blake to see. Come was now running down my legs.

"You never loved me, did you? You couldn't have. You don't do stuff like this to someone you love. It was all a game for you."

Drake didn't respond.

"You were willing to share me with your

brother. *What if your cell hadn't gone off? Would you have compared notes? Would this have been your private joke or were you planning to join in? Am I just a joke to you? Am I, Drake?"*

Drake and Blake looked at me like I was totally pathetic.

"It doesn't even matter. Just go," I said, defeated.

"Are you going to call the police?"

By now, Drake's words were like a haze of non-sense. I continued to rock and wipe tears from my eyes.

I responded with one word. *"No."*

"Good girl," Drake stated, smiling for the first time.

"No one would believe this," I whispered, wiping away tears with the back of my hand. *"How could I be such a fool?"*

Drake and Blake quietly and quickly let themselves out and I lay on top of my bed and drifted off to sleep. I didn't have the ability to pull any cover over myself. My mind couldn't function any longer or begin to comprehend what had happened.

The next day I woke up around noon. I completely blocked out everything that had happened from the previous night. I did two loads of laundry and even ran a few errands. I tossed all the bed linen, including my gown, into a big garbage bag and trashed it. I think I even stopped by Mother's house and talked and smiled like all was good in my life.

Later that day, I had a couple of phone hang ups. My phone would ring and once I answered it, the person on the other line wouldn't say anything, or the person would hold the line. All I'd hear would be breathing. Finally, I turned off the ringer in order to get some peace and I turned off my cell phone. Glancing out the window, I thought I saw an SUV that looked like Drake's drive slowly by. I quickly dismissed the image to my overactive imagination and moved away from the window. Much later that evening, I cooked some spaghetti and made a tossed salad. I ate a late meal all alone.

Other than that, the day after was just like any other day. In my mind, anyway. What makes one want to take their own life? Now I know. Wisdom has a way of slipping up on you when you don't even realize you've recognized it. When you've been humiliated beyond repair, when you have nothing to wake up for, when living is a chore, when all your realities are lies, that's when God has given you more than you can handle and the will to live has vanished like a thief in the night.

Chapter 25

It was the Saturday after running into Drake and Blake on Thursday at work. Friday was another day I spent in bed, buried under my covers and trying to hide from the truth. I would learn that the truth has a way of finding you. I was still in bed even though I had been awake for a couple of hours, but I couldn't muster up the energy to move. Just the simple task of going to the bathroom took every ounce of energy I possessed. My phones had rung on and off over the last day and a half, but I just let the voice mails pick up. I didn't want to be bothered. I couldn't deal with anything or anyone. Not now.

Finally, around noon, I forced myself to get up. I felt like an old lady; my steps were slow and measured. I slowly made a trek for the bathroom and relieved myself. I looked a straight mess when I saw my reflection in the mirror. My hair looked like a bird's nest and a bird's family had taken residence, and I desperately needed a long, hot shower. I smelled myself so I knew I stank.

Once in the shower, I found myself shedding even more tears. I thought I was all cried out over the entire mess. I didn't know if they were tears of shame, humiliation, loss, or despair. I felt all alone in the world. My biological mom threw me away and now Drake thought I was dispensable too. All the people I thought loved and cared for me had let me down. That's why I didn't bring too many people in. They always disappointed.

I briefly thought of calling Mother, but she wouldn't understand and she'd want to fix things, but there was no way that this could ever be repaired. No amount of hot soup, pampering, and moving back in with me could fix this. This was beyond repair. Plus, I didn't want to spoil Mother's newfound happiness. I couldn't put her through this. This was my mess and these were the consequences of my bad decisions and misjudgment of character.

I stayed in the shower until the water turned cold. Stepping out, cold and shivering, I slowly dressed in wrinkled jeans, and a black wife beater and black jogging shoes. I pulled my hair back into a messy ponytail, secured it with a scrunchie, and managed to eat a cold sandwich and drink a soda. I was simply functioning on memory and routine. After those tasks were completed, I didn't know what to do with myself.

I didn't want to think. I didn't want to move. I didn't want to even be me. I sat on the patio and stared at the neighborhood like I was seeing it for the first time. I observed people going about their everyday lives. There were some families who were happily smiling and laughing as they went their merry way. Children were riding their bikes on the sidewalk, laughing and having a great time with not a care in the world. A few neighbors were leisurely walking their pets and enjoying the new day, and a few young men were washing their rides, getting them ready for the weekend and probably a date. Others were jogging. Life went on. No one knew, or cared, what I'd been through. It's true: *life doesn't stop for your problems*.

As I sat there, my thoughts went to Mother. A few days earlier, we'd finally had the talk. I expressed to her my desire to find my birth mom.

I phoned Taylor and told her I planned to talk to mother after church; Taylor gave me a pep talk and I was ready. As ready as I would be.

Mother and I had eaten and were sitting in her living room. The TV was on but we weren't really watching anything in particular. I think she was working on a crossword puzzle and I was content to be in her presence.

"Pastor preached a great sermon today, don't you think?" she asked, glancing over at me.

I nodded.

"Finding self-love is vital to being happy in life. We have to love ourselves before we should expect anyone else to. God wants us to live the best lives we can and to be the best person we can be."

"Mother, I have something I need to talk to you about," I said, abruptly changing the subject.

"Sure, sweetie," she said, closing the crossword puzzle book. I guess she sensed this was important.

"I, well, you know that I love you."

"I do."

"I love you and Daddy so much and I appreciate everything you've done for me over the years. I couldn't ask for better parents."

"Thank you, sweetie. I appreciate that."

"But . . ."

"But what?" I had her undivided attention but couldn't get the words out. Then Taylor's words

popped into my mind. Mother wanted me to be happy. It was that simple.

"I would like to find my birth mother."

She paused for only a second.

"And I want you to find her. I know you have questions, questions that neither your daddy nor I can answer. I knew this time would come soon or later. I have some paperwork I can give you to aid in your search. I kept it thinking it might come in handy one day."

"Are up mad?"

"Sweetie, absolutely not. Is that what you think? Is that what's bothering you?"

"I don't know what I think anymore."

"Well, let me tell you. Since the first time I saw you, you have brought nothing but joy into my life. I'm not so selfish that I don't want you to be whole and complete. If this will bring you peace and a sense of completeness, please look for her. Just know that I love you more than life itself."

With that, a heavy burden was lifted off my shoulders because I knew I had her blessings.

I thought back to a phone call I had received a few days after our conversation and I still wasn't sure how I felt about it or what I was going to do. No one but me was aware of the call because I hadn't shared it with Mother, Daddy, or Taylor yet. I had picked up the call, not immediately recognizing the phone number displayed.

"May I speak with Kennedy Logan, please?"

"This is Kennedy."

"Hi. This is Beverly Jenkins at Boleman Detective Agency and Mr. Jackson asked me to give you a call

because he is going to be out of the loop for a couple of hours, in a meeting."

"Okay," I stated, waiting for her to continue.

"We have some wonderful news to share. Are you sitting down?" she asked excitedly.

"I am now," I stated with a slight tremble to my voice.

"We found your birth mother, Kennedy."

I exhaled, not even realizing I had been holding my breath up until that point.

"Wow." That was all I could think to whisper.

"I know this must be overwhelming news. We were able to locate her quickly based on the information you supplied. You can come into the office and we will give you all the details, or, if you prefer, I can give you the details over the phone right now, Kennedy. It's totally your decision."

"No, I'm fine with receiving the information over the phone. Let me grab a pen and paper."

"Sure. Take your time."

"Okay, I'm back."

"Are you ready?" Beverly asked.

"As ready as I will ever be," I stated, taking a deep breath.

"Your birth mother's name is Jennifer Coleman and she lives at . . ."

And that is how I heard my birth mother's name for the first time. I was provided with her full address and a phone number with a few other details. I remember slowly hanging up the phone, literally trembling and crying and laughing and not understanding the overwhelming emotions I was feeling. They were all over the place. I sat on the sofa with the piece of paper in my hand, staring at it in disbelief, and read my birth mom's name and information over and again. It was all surreal.

I had been sitting for about an hour when my phone rang. I still hadn't bothered to check the messages from the day before. On impulse and habit I picked up my cordless phone since it was lying right beside me.

"Hello?"

"Hey, baby."

I froze.

"Hello. I know you're there."

I still didn't speak. I couldn't if I wanted to. I'm not sure if I was even breathing.

"Listen, Blake and I really want to drop by and make amends."

Silence.

"Maybe we can take you out to lunch, or perhaps you could fix us something at your place. We want to get past this and move on."

I didn't have the strength to hang up.

"Blake will be leaving tomorrow for LA and we wanted to hang out with you for a minute.

"Kennedy, please say something. Anything. I love you. Please give me one more chance. I made a huge mistake, but I realize now how much I truly love you. I always did, but I was scared of those feelings; terrified of committing."

My entire body was visibly shaking, and I think I started hysterically laughing as I held the phone away from my ear.

"Okay, don't say anything. We're on our way over. We'll talk then. Just the three of us."

I immediately threw the phone down, ran into the living room, and grabbed my purse. All I could think about was getting out of the apartment. On autopilot, I sprinted out my front door, bolted to my car, and drove out of the parking lot like a bat out of hell. Tires squealing.

Now, I had been aimlessly riding around for about two hours. I didn't know where I was going; I only knew that I had to get away. I couldn't be there when Drake and Blake showed up. No way. I couldn't believe this was happening and had no idea how to stop it. That was the sad part.

I retrieved my cell phone and thought briefly of calling Mother. I had succeeded in dialing three of digits of her phone number when I cleared the call from my cell phone. Mother had done so much for me. I didn't want her to be disappointed in me. I glanced down at the dashboard and noticed I was low on gas, so I pulled off at the next exit and purchased a tank of gas and a soda.

After getting back on the interstate, I drove a couple of miles up the road and pulled off at a rest stop. I sat in the car, away from all the other travelers, trying to free my mind enough to think. My heartbeat had finally slowed back to normal. When I first heard Drake's voice, I thought my heart would jump out of my chest. I still couldn't rationalize how a person could be so heartless. And, better yet, why I hadn't seen him for what he truly was.

I sat at the rest stop for about thirty minutes, going over all my options. Reliving that night, rewinding it over and fast-forwarding it in my head. Trying to determine if I knew at any point that Blake wasn't Drake. Trying to figure out what signals I was sending out to men to make them think they could treat me like I didn't matter. The last serious relationship I had, my boyfriend cheated on me at least three times that I was aware of. I'm sure there were others that I just didn't know about. When we broke up because our relationship had become a bad joke, Kenny informed me that I was too emotionally needy. I drained him. He said he couldn't be my lover and my father. I thought about that now.

Finally, in a flash of clarity I knew what had to be done. I understood what I had to do. I had one phone call left to make. Before I lost my nerve, I dialed Taylor's number. Surprisingly, she picked up on the second ring.

"Kennedy?"

"Yeah, it's me."

"K, where are you?"

"It doesn't matter."

"You had us so worried. Your mother has been trying to reach you for twenty-four hours now. And I drove by your apartment this afternoon and your front door was partially open. I locked up for you and closed your patio door."

"Thanks."

"K, what's going on? I'm scared."

"So am I," I whispered.

"I talked to your next-door neighbor and she said she noticed some strange man has been watching your apartment. Yesterday, he approached her asking fifty questions. He fits Drake's description."

"It doesn't even matter anymore."

"It does matter. K, where are you?"

"Taylor, I'm going away for a while," I stated calmly.

"What? Going where? Come home, come stay with me and let's talk about this some more."

"No, there's nothing to talk about. Nothing to say. I want to thank you for being such a good friend to me all these years."

"K, you're scaring me. Just come home," she cried out to me.

"Don't be scared. This is for the best. Tell Mother not to worry and tell her that I love her," I said with a trembling voice.

"Why can't you tell her? You come home and tell her."

"I can't right now. And, Taylor, I've always loved you, too. I've always admired you and wanted to be like you. I'm so proud of your strength and determination. You've been like a sister to me."

"Kennedy, we are proud of you too and I love you so much." Taylor was openly sobbing now.

"I've got to go," I stated firmly before I changed my mind.

"No, not yet. Wait."

"No, I've said what I needed to say. I just called to say I love you and to thank you for being my friend. Don't worry about me. Now, I have to go."

"K, it can't be that bad."

"It is. It's worse. It's worse than you can ever imagine."

By now, Taylor's sobs were even louder. They broke my heart into pieces.

"Drake set it up for his brother, Blake, to rape me." There, I'd said it. I acknowledged it for the first time. It felt so strange coming off my lips and out of my mouth. It was like I was talking about someone else. That couldn't have possibly happened to me.

"What? Please tell me I heard you wrong."

"You didn't."

"Kennedy, I'm so sorry. I never knew Drake was that demented and, oh my God, this is what you've been dealing with. Why didn't you call the police, or why didn't you call me?"

"I don't know. I thought if I didn't say it out loud, it would go away. Yet, I live it over and over again. It won't go away. It has destroyed my life. Those images, his smell . . ."

"Sweetie, come home. We love you. We'll work through this somehow. I'll personally take you down to the police station. Take some time off from work. We'll get you into a rape survivor program."

"No. It's too late, Taylor. And there's more."

"What? You can tell me anything. I'm always in your corner and it's never, ever too late."

"Back in January, I didn't really have the flu. I tried to kill myself. I overdosed on some pills."

"Oh, Kennedy. I didn't know. I didn't know. Tell me, what can I do to help?"

"Now you know. Now you know everything."

"We can get you through this. You have so many people who love and care about you. People who are in your corner. Drake is sick. What happened has nothing to do with you, sweetie."

"No, no one can help me. I can't even help myself. Goodbye, Taylor."

I disconnected the line, turned off my cell, and continued driving away from everyone who loved me. Around nightfall, I pulled into the parking lot of a motel, right outside Chattanooga, Tennessee. I paid the front desk person for one night, retrieved my key, and walked to my room. I knew what I had to do. For once, everything was all so clear. Crystal clear.

Chapter 26

Over at Kennedy's apartment, the early Sunday morning rays and sounds stirred Dorothy and Taylor. Not that they had gotten much sleep anyway because they had tried to stay up in case Kennedy called back or needed them. They had finally dozed off around daybreak, when their minds absolutely refused to function any longer.

Earlier, after talking back and forth with one another, they decided to set up at Kennedy's apartment. A neighbor was staying over at Dorothy's home in case she showed up there. The police had been notified, but they were no help. They explained that an adult had to be missing for twenty-four hours before they'd declare them as missing and be able to investigate. Dorothy and Taylor didn't want to entertain the thought that in twenty-four hours, it might be too late.

Mr. Logan was expected to arrive at Hartsfield-Jackson International Airport that morning. A buddy was picking him up and dropping him off at the apartment. That way, no one had to leave the house, or phone duty. He had been informed of the situation and finally told of the chain of the events that transpired at the first of the year.

Even though he was disappointed that it had been kept from him, he put his hurt aside and concentrated on the safe return of his daughter. He held back his intense anger, temporarily, to seek out, find, and murder Drake with his bare hands. For now, they decided not to inform the police of the rape. Their total focus was on guaranteeing Kennedy's safe return home.

After Taylor's brief phone contact with Kennedy, they hadn't heard another single word. Kennedy's cell phone had been turned off and her voice mail was full of their urgent requests for her to call home. They couldn't leave any more messages. Calls had been made the previous night to various people, and Taylor had even driven around town checking out hotels and different spots in hopes of spotting Kennedy's car. All to no avail.

As much as it took every ounce of control she had in her to be civil, Taylor called Drake and asked if he had heard anything from Kennedy. He said he hadn't. Of course, his arrogant ass was of no additional help. He was clueless. He didn't even realize what a chain effect his actions had caused. Now, they were simply playing the waiting game. With each passing hour, the tension in the apartment thickened. It was so thick it was almost suffocating.

Kennedy's presence was everywhere in the apartment. Her books, candles, and her perfume scent were all constant reminders. A couple of times, telemarketing calls came in that they rushed to answer, only to be disappointed by someone trying to sell a product or service.

Both Dorothy and Taylor had fallen asleep in the living room, on the sofas, fully dressed. Light throws shrouded each of them. Neither one wanted to be too far away from the front door. They wanted to be there with open arms when Kennedy walked through it. Also, if they were totally honest and admitted it, they needed to draw on each other's comfort and silent strength. They were trying to act brave for each other. However, it was only that. An act. No one wanted to think of what could happen to Kennedy in her present state of mind. They refused to consider that viable option. Kennedy was fragile. She always had been emotionally fragile.

Around eight A.M. the ringing doorbell awakened them from their fretful sleep. They each dreamed similar scenarios of silent cries for help from a shadowed female and being unable, but willing, to do anything. Their feet strangely cemented in place, they were unable to offer any assistance and could only look on helplessly. The doorbell was a welcomed relief; Dorothy woke up first and raced to answer the door. She hadn't displayed that much energy and speed since the events unraveled.

She slung open the door expecting and hoping to see her beloved daughter. It never crossed her tired mind that Kennedy wouldn't be ringing her own doorbell. She'd simply use her key, unlock the door, and walk in.

Dorothy opened the door and came face-to-face with Mr. Logan for the first time in years. His eyes held such sadness and pain. Suddenly, fresh tears that could no longer be contained burst forth in their eyes. Mr. Logan took that first step over the threshold. No words were spoken. Dorothy simply fell into his open and comforting arms. The events of the past didn't matter. Now, it was all about Kennedy. The one person and subject they totally agreed on. If nothing else, their love for her was true and valid.

"It's going to be all right. Don't cry, darling. We'll

find our girl," Mr. Logan chanted over and over again. "We'll get through this . . . together."

"Come sit down," he stated, leading Dorothy gently to the sofa because she had totally collapsed against him. His strong presence allowed Dorothy to give in for a moment to her true feelings. She leaned against Robert's solid chest. He'd always been her foundation, the strength she drew from.

"Hello, Mr. Logan," Taylor stated quietly, breaking the spell.

"Hey, Taylor. How ya been, baby? I hate that we have to see each other again under these circumstances. Have y'all heard anything else?" he asked, looking from one to the other with expectant eyes.

Taylor's eyes were red rimmed and puffy from a long night of crying. "No, sir. Nothing."

"Well, guess what? We aren't going to have all these sad faces in here. No, sir. Dorothy, Taylor, I want you to gather around in a circle and join hands. We're going to say a prayer and ask God to protect my baby and lead and guide her through this dark moment in her life."

Everybody stood up, joined hands, and closed their eyes with bowed heads. Mr. Logan led the powerful, heartfelt prayer.

"Dear merciful God and my personal savior, we are standing here today asking and praying that you'll protect our daughter and friend. Keep Kennedy in your protective arms and embrace. Guide her, lead her, and shield her. Dear Heavenly Father, help my daughter to understand that you'll never forsake her. No matter how lonely she may be feeling, no matter how bleak her situation may seem, no matter what life throws her way, you're there, right beside her. Carrying her when she can't walk. Being her strength and calm in the storm. Keep her from harm's way, dear God. Let her feel the strong arms of our love reaching out to her, calling and guiding her safely back to us. Let her know that her family loves her no matter what. That will never change.

"Heavenly Father, protect my baby girl. Let her realize how precious she is to us, our gift. Oh, Father, make us strong, when we are worn down. Give us the strength to get through this storm. Keep us faithful and steadfast in knowing you'll return Kennedy safe and sound to us. We ask for forgiveness in our hearts against those who have harmed our baby. Cloak her in love and protection, Lord. These things we ask in your name, Amen."

"Amen," Dorothy and Taylor stated in unison. They believed in the power of prayer.

Everyone had tears in their eyes. Yet, a powerful force was felt throughout the room. Hope wasn't lost. Hope was alive and well. In order to keep busy, Dorothy folded the blankets, put them away, then showed Mr. Logan where he could place his belongings and freshen up.

"It's good to see you, old man."

"You too, Dorothy. You haven't changed. Still as lovely as ever."

Self-consciously, she touched her hair. Linking her arm through his, she stated, "Well, you, old man, need to get a shave and shower so that you won't frighten our daughter when she walks through that front door and sees you."

"Oh, I don't look that bad, do I?" They both laughed. It felt good.

"No, actually you're a sight for sore eyes," Dorothy said seriously, gently patting his arm.

"It's been a long time, Dorothy," Robert stated, staring into her eyes. Old feelings resurfaced.

"Yes, it has."

"You go do what you need to. The towels are in the linen closet in the hallway and the bar soap is under the sink."

"Thanks, Dorothy."

"No, thank you for being here."

"I wouldn't have had it any other way. That's our daughter out there."

"Well, I'm going to start dinner because I know that child is going to be starving when she walks through that door. I'll fix her favorites and have them ready for her when she comes home."

"You do that. You always were a good mother."

"Robert, she is walking through that door, isn't she?"

"What do you think?"

There was a silent confirmation that Kennedy would return unharmed, physically anyway.

"After you take a shower and freshen up, we need to talk. Our baby is in trouble and we need to come up with a plan to see her through this."

"I can't believe you and Kennedy kept her suicide attempt from me. All those times I spoke with her and she pretended everything was okay. I can only imagine the pain she has been hiding and feeling."

"Kennedy has always been good at masking her feelings, even as a child."

"I should have been here for her," Robert stated, hanging his head.

"Well, you are now. That's what counts. Now, go freshen up."

"Okay."

"Robert?"

"Huh?"

"Again, it's good having you here. I mean that."

"It's good being here, with you. I just hate the circumstances."

"I know, but God will see us through this."

"Amen."

Taylor had excused herself to Kennedy's bedroom so that she wouldn't interfere with the mini-reunion going on in the living room. She felt closer to her friend there. Taylor was exhausted mentally, physically, and emotionally. She tried Kennedy's cell phone number, but once again received the voice mail. Kennedy's voice sounded so happy on the tape. Her laughter was always music to her ears. Taylor even checked her voice mail at home. Nothing. Where could she be? And what was her present state of mind?

As the small apartment took on a life of its own, everyone settled in for a long day. Preparations were being made for when Kennedy walked through the door.

Chapter 27

It was early Sunday morning and I had been sitting in my car outside the modest stucco-framed home with blue trim for over an hour. Watching, sitting, and thinking as I sipped soda from a straw. The house sat nestled in an older, quiet neighborhood. So far, I hadn't noticed any activity within its walls. All was quiet. I'd double-checked the address at least three times; I wanted to make sure that this was indeed the place. The home of my birth mom, Jennifer Coleman.

Over two weeks ago, I had received information on her from the search agency I'd hired. I didn't tell Mother or Taylor of my find because I wasn't sure what I was going to do with it. A part of me longed to know my background and to meet the woman who gave birth to me. I wanted—no, needed—answers.

On the other hand, I was afraid of what answers and truths I might receive and if I could handle them. Or worse yet, if I was rejected again. This Jennifer Coleman wasn't aware that I was paying an unannounced visit. This entire moment felt like a Lifetime movie of the week. I didn't realize how nervous I was until I glanced down at my hands; they were shaking uncontrollably.

Yesterday, without my consciously realizing it, I found myself driving toward Johnson City, Tennessee. I was on autopilot most of the drive; my thoughts all

over the place. I couldn't think straight. Too much had
happened over the last few days. After checking into a
motel on the outskirts of town, I spent the remainder
of the night reflecting upon my life. I had turned off my
cell phone so I wouldn't be disturbed. I needed to do
some serious thinking and be alone with my thoughts.
I made a promise to myself, sitting cross-legged in the
middle of the bed. I wasn't going to run any longer. I
had been running my entire life, and it was time to be
still and find peace; find that self-love.

Late that evening I ate chili, fries, and a side salad
from a Wendy's down the street. I woke up at the crack
of dawn from a restless sleep, and started my journey.
It was spectacular to see the sun, in all its blazing glory,
rise above the horizon to start another day. I took
that as a sign that today would be the beginning of a
new start for me. Along the way, I cried some more. I
grieved the love I thought I had and then I felt my heart
discard it. I deserved better and henceforth would demand better. It's true; a person will only treat you bad
if you let them.

I stopped at a McDonald's to get a soda and sausage
biscuit and continued on my way. I had driven for
about two hours when I realized I did need to make
another phone call. It was after our song came on the
radio. I composed myself after another bout of crying
and pulled over at the next rest stop, which was three
miles down the interstate, and pulled out my cell. It
was getting low on battery power.

I prayed. Prayed some more. Then, I called Drake.
Called him for the last time. I slowly pushed each digit
of his number like I had done hundreds of times before. The phone rang and rang and rang with no pickup

other than his voice mail. It didn't matter. It was probably for the best.

I wanted to get this off my chest and it didn't matter if I told Drake face-to-face, over the phone, or in an impersonal voice mail. Who knew when Drake would arrive home; he was probably still out partying from the night before, or laid up with somebody. I listened to his voice. Closed my eyes to commit it to memory. He always had such a sexy, deep voice. One day he would miss me and realize how wrong he was. One day he'd be sorry. One day he would get a dose of his own medicine.

My message, which took two phone calls, went like this:

"Drake, I want to inform you that you are not going to intimidate, harass, or threaten me anymore. Do you hear me? I'm sick of running. I've prayed about you. Today, I made the decision to fight. If you ever call me, drive by, or come near my apartment again, I swear I will call the police and report you. Everything will come out. Everything. I have no more to lose.

"One day, you'll get yours, because we really do reap what we sow. I deserved so much more from you. I loved you. Thought you were the one. The man of my dreams. Now, I just pity you. I pity you. Don't ever contact me again. I realize you tried to shape me into someone I wasn't, tried to strip away my self-esteem, take away something that was precious to me. You almost succeeded, but not quite, because I'm still standing. I'm still standing. Good-bye, Drake."

After hanging up, I felt free. Free like a bird gliding through the sky. I felt like a burden had been released from my shoulders, and when I turned back on the radio, an oldie was playing. "Jesus Walks," by Kanye West. For the remainder of my drive, I felt confident that no matter what went down, I knew I could handle it. I *was* stronger than I thought. I was humiliated, and had almost sacrificed my soul for a man, but I was still standing. He couldn't steal my joy. A calmness settled over me and I sensed a shroud of protection and love surrounding me. I was at peace.

It was now or never. It was time to meet my birth mom. Time to come face-to-face with the woman who gave me away twenty-eight years ago. I checked myself in the rearview mirror, opened the car door, inched out, and slowly made my way up the narrow, cracked walkway. Each step I took gave me another ounce of confidence. I arrived at the front door, brushed my hair in place, took a quick breath, and knocked. I wasn't sure what to expect, but I was finally ready.

A few seconds later, a middle-aged woman with a pink and white duster on answered with a puzzled look on her face. The smell of breakfast cooking drifted out to greet my nose. There was no question about it, the woman standing before me was definitely my mom. We shared the same eyes, lips, and nose. She had the type of fading beauty where you could tell she had seen a hard life. I blinked back tears.

We studied each other for only seconds before I spoke first, but it seemed liked hours. I witnessed her face go through various states of emotion as she slowly realized who I was.

"I'm Kennedy Logan and I'm your daughter."

She inhaled and let her breath back out slowly.

"Kennedy. Such a beautiful name for a beautiful girl. I always wondered what they'd name you," she whispered.

"Are you Jennifer Coleman?"

"Yes. Kennedy, I've been waiting for this moment all my life. I've dreamed about this very second. And look at me. My hair is a mess and I'm walking around in a dirty old duster with holes," she stated, trying to brush her hair in place.

"Don't worry, I won't take up too much of your time. I have a few questions I'd like to ask," I stated in a flat monotone. I didn't recognize my own voice.

"Look at you."

I just stood there, devoid of any emotion.

"May we talk?" I asked in a professional tone.

"Of course, of course," she cried and burst into tears.

After that, she grabbed me into an embrace. At first, I froze, and then my arms slowly rose to encircle her thin, shuddering shoulders. I held on for dear life and we both cried and cried and cried. We softly sobbed until there were no tears left. We must have been a sight to her neighbors. It was such an emotional cleansing that I didn't care. I could have stood there all day, locked in her arms.

We finally pulled away and stood back to shyly check each other out again.

"I've missed you," she whispered. "I've missed you so much right here," she said, pointing to her heart.

I realized in that moment that I had as well. "I've missed you too."

"Come on in here. You're just in time; I was fixing myself some country grits, scrambled eggs, and ham. Sundays are the only morning I get to prepare breakfast for myself. I eat and sit around all day catching up on my reading and watching classic movies."

I hesitated.

"Come on. Don't be scared. You didn't come here for nothing. I have so much to tell you."

I slowly walked through the door and looked around curiously at my surroundings. The living room didn't contain many photos or artwork. It was decorated very modestly. As I could tell from the outside, this wasn't a large home. It was cozy, though, and possessed a warm, lived-in feeling.

"Follow me. The kitchen is right through here. Try to overlook my mess. As I said, most Sundays I just laze around and it's only me."

She paused to look back at me. "You know, you look just like me when I was your age."

"Do I?" I asked, still checking out my surroundings.

"You're twenty-eight, aren't you?"

"Yes."

We made it to the kitchen and she immediately went back to the stove and finished cooking while I sat in a chair at the small, well-worn table. I could tell she was glad to have something to do to occupy her hands. With her back to me, I could really look at her. We had the same general build and frame.

"Relax, relax. Later, I'll show you some photos of your relatives."

"I'd like that."

"You are so polite and pretty. I knew you'd turn out fine. I prayed constantly for it."

I sat at the small oak table and watched her move around the kitchen with a swiftness. A hot plate was soon passed my way. The food looked delicious, but I wasn't hungry. I wanted answers.

"Thank you."

"I don't have any orange juice or coffee, but I do have

a can of soda that you're welcome to share. I know most people don't drink soda for—"

In spite of myself, I laughed, "Soda is fine."

She gave me a curious look.

I tried to explain. "I'm sorry. It's a private joke. Now, I know you really are my mom."

We ate breakfast in a tension-filled silence. Raw emotions were slicing the air. Not many words were spoken. We knew questions and answers would come later. I ate, but I never tasted the food. Finally, breakfast was finished, plates were stacked in the sink, we moved to the sparse living room, and I received long-awaited answers. I didn't hold back. I came out swinging. I didn't have time to beat around the bush. I had waited too many years and beat myself up, thinking I was worthless and not valued.

"Why did you give me up? Why didn't you love me?"

"Baby, I've always loved you. I've thought about you every second, every minute, every day of my existence. I wanted you to have a better life than me. I needed you to experience a grander life than I could give you. I couldn't even take care of myself, let alone a baby."

"All a child needs is love. That's all."

"Did you receive that?" she asked, looking me up and down.

"Yes, I felt very loved growing up, but I could have gotten that from you too. Even with love, I could never get past feeling unwanted by you."

"I'm sorry. I'm truly sorry. But, baby, I didn't even love myself and I didn't want you growing up in my environment. It was a living hell."

"Why didn't you come looking for me?"

"I figured you were better off where you were. Kennedy,

I work as a waitress at a restaurant. This tiny house is the only thing I've ever owned in my entire life and I've scrimped and saved for it. It's been a struggle. But it's mine. I never had any more children. I've never married. I'm surviving paycheck to paycheck. You didn't need me back in your life. I figured if you ever wanted to know me, you'd find me. And hopefully, by then, you'd have a reason to be proud of me."

I looked down at my hands.

"But I never stopped, not for one second, loving you or thinking about you. Please believe me," she said, looking deep within my soul. And for some reason, I believed her.

"What happened?" I asked quietly. "What was so wrong in your life?"

"It's a long story. Let me get a smoke and I'll explain everything," she stated with trembling hands.

My biological mom retrieved her cigarettes from a worn purse lying on the coffee table, and for the next three hours, I listened to her heartbreaking story. I heard for the first time the tale of a young girl from the wrong side of the tracks who fell for a married, older man who promised her the world, but the girl got pregnant, the man abandoned her almost immediately, and she knew she couldn't raise a baby in her dysfunctional, drug-infested home. So, she did a noble thing and gave the baby up for adoption, in hopes of her daughter having a better life than she could ever give her or hope for.

I learned about my biological maternal family. My grandparents were dead, but I had one aunt who lived not too far from there. I heard my father's name for the first time. Supposedly, he was still married with a family of his own. She never heard from him again and never sought him out. Just lived with the heartache and buried a part of herself in the process.

Slowly, I released all the pain; some I didn't know existed until that very moment. It was a very emotional but cleansing day. Almost like a rebirth. I felt I would never be the same again; I valued myself with a newness I had never appreciated. After exchanging phone numbers and promising to visit again, the first thing I did after walking out the door was to pick up the phone and call Mother. Later, I found out she had her calls forwarded to my house.

The phone rang only once. Mother picked up right away, breathlessly.

"Mother?"

"Oh, thank God. Thank you, Jesus. Lord, you answered my prayers," she screamed into the receiver.

"Mother?"

"Yes, baby, it's Mother. I'm right here. Where are you? Are you all right? You didn't hurt yourself?"

"No, I'm fine. I'm ready to come home now. I'm sorry that I had you worried and upset. I wasn't thinking rationally. I didn't even realize I was—"

"It's okay, baby. Come home, because we're more than ready to see you."

"We?"

"Yes, Taylor and your father are here, waiting for you."

"I'm so sorry that I worried everybody. I didn't mean to—"

"Don't think about that now. Come home, baby. We love you."

"Okay."

"Do we need to pick you up from somewhere?"

"No, I can make it. I have my car."

"Kennedy, I love you so much and just the thought that I had lost you . . ."

"Mother, I'm fine, better than fine, and I promise I'll never scare you like this again."

"You better not. Hold on, your daddy wants to talk with you."

"Okay."

"Hey there, sweet darling."

"Hey, Daddy."

"You gave us quite a scare, but you come on home now and stop all this nonsense. Your mother has prepared all your favorite dishes and I can't wait to give you a big hug and kiss. You hear me?"

"I hear you." I couldn't help but smile.

"I love you, baby."

"Love you, too."

"We'll see you soon, sweetie. Drive carefully. Hold on again, Taylor is reaching for the phone."

"Girl, if you ever scare me like this again. I swear I'm going to—"

"Kill me?" I asked. "You know you can say the word around me."

She laughed. "What are we going to do with you?" she cried out in joy. "My Kennedy."

"I'm sorry, Taylor. I didn't mean to put you through this."

"Just come home, K, to where you belong."

"I will."

"And K?"

"Huh?"

"I love you, girl. Always have."

"Me too."

I hung up the phone with a big grin on my face. A real genuine smile, the first one in a long time. I sensed everything really was going to be okay. I turned on my car and I headed home. Home to where I was very loved.

Epilogue

Approximately a year later

Dear Journal,

It's a year after one of the worst times of my life. I've learned so many lessons about myself, about love and relationships, and about family. I've grown to appreciate all the good things and wonderful people in my life. I count my blessings each and every day. Maybe God doesn't give us more than we can handle. I'm still standing. I'm definitely a stronger and wiser person. And time does help with healing our hurts.

A lot has changed around here, but change is good sometimes. Believe it or not, I'm back at home for a little while. A little while being not over two years. After discussing it with Mother and Daddy, we agreed it'd be cheaper for me to live at home and attend school. Yes, I'm back in school, working on a MBA. I never returned to my old employer because it would be too uncomfortable for me there. Too many whispers when I walked in a room. Now, I work part time, in customer service, for a smaller company, until I graduate with my advanced degree. Once a week I go to counseling for my feelings regarding the rape *and my suicide attempt, and it's helping make my healing process smoother. I am not alone.*

I'm learning to appreciate myself and put my needs and myself first. And you know what, it feels wonderful. Taylor and I treat ourselves to a spa day at least once a month. We indulge in everything from massages, and body wraps, to facials, manicures, and pedicures. Our friendship has grown even stronger during this ordeal. I've finally come to understand that Taylor doesn't judge and loves me for me.

Michael, my previous coworker, and I casually date. Nothing serious. We go out to the movies or dinner now and then. We talk on the phone maybe once a week; he keeps me laughing. He's a really nice and decent man. It's about time I met one. I didn't know they existed. And to think, he was right there under my nose the entire time. He respects my decision to be celibate for a while; he simply enjoys spending time with me and vice versa. I don't know if Michael is the man for me, but I know whoever steals my heart will see a more confident woman.

Mother and Daddy reconciled and got back together, but I guess you suspected that. They remarried, went on a second honeymoon to Hawaii, and could not be happier. Mother still dotes on Daddy too much until he tells her to stop. And guess what? She listens. They are both trying not to make the same mistakes they made the first time around. Communication channels are open. They are adorable. When anyone asks how they are doing, they give a secretive smile and say,

"It's better the second time around." I watch them and look forward to someday meeting my life-long mate. I know he's out there somewhere.

Taylor is still diva Taylor. I love that girl like a sister. She and Mr. Attorney are still hanging strong. I can't believe it because this is a record for her. I have to admit, though, Walter is a super nice guy. And she received another promotion. Taylor is doing her thing and having tons of fun in the process. That's what I love about her. She's a beautiful, intelligent, and down-to-earth black woman who has it going on. Taylor knows what she wants out of life and she goes for it. She's fierce.

Drake. I never saw him again. I never received an apology or an explanation. It doesn't matter. Drake got his due justice. Like they say, every dog has its day. After allegations of sexual harassment and inappropriate behavior on his part from at least half a dozen women surfaced, he resigned before they fired his sorry ass. After discovering his other women on the side, I heard Brittany led the crusade against him. Women were coming out of the woodwork with their se-duction stories. All concerned parties quietly set-tled out of court. My settlement was inner peace and joy.

Last I heard, Drake's back in Los Angeles, but who knows, and I really don't care. Rumor has it that he had previously tried the same mess at his family-owned business. That's why his parents shipped him to Atlanta after settling out of court over similar nonsense. So, he still didn't learn the lesson.

I know he didn't get exactly what he deserved. Blake either. But I sincerely believe that their day will come. Drake and Blake have some issues to iron out with women. You can't use and abuse women and not have to pay repercussions at some point. One day, they will meet the wrong one and there will be hell to pay. I just want to be a fly on the wall when the shit hits the fan.

As for my birth mom, I'm learning more and more about her as time goes on. I now understand the enormous pressure she was under. All the chips were definitely stacked against her and my aunt, Louise. I think she made a wise and unselfish decision in placing me for adoption. We don't speak each and every day, but we do make time for each other. She and Mother and Daddy have met and they hit it off okay. I wasn't expecting instant friendship or connections. I think they realize what they don't have in common, they make up for by loving me. I couldn't ask for more.

These are my true confessions, 2010.

Questions for Discussion

1. What were Kennedy's issues that prohibited her from having a healthy relationship with Drake and previous boyfriends?

2. Do you feel she was in love with Drake?

3. What are your thoughts regarding Drake? Was he a womanizer?

4. Did he care at all for Kennedy or was he using her?

5. How did you feel about the different relationship storylines presented? Kennedy and Drake? Kennedy and Taylor? Kennedy and her mother? Kennedy and her father?

6. Was Taylor a good friend? Do you feel Kennedy was attracted to her because she was all the things she wasn't?

7. How did Kennedy's feelings of abandonment by her birth mother play into her insecurities and low self-esteem?

8. Are you adopted or do you know someone who is?

Do you feel there is a natural inclination to want to know your roots?

9. Why do you feel Drake was attracted to Kennedy to begin with? Do you think he was addicted to sex?

10. Did you think Kennedy's reasons for attempted suicide were valid? Have you ever thought of or known anyone who committed suicide?

11. Do you think suicide is a sin?

12. What did you think about Kennedy's final confession? Do you think she somehow blamed herself?

13. What is your true confession? Do you feel confession is good for the soul?

14. What did you think of the sexual scenes? Did they add flavor to or take away from the storyline?

15. What do you foresee in Kennedy's future? In her parents' future?